The House That Ate People

The House That Ate People

Dayle Courtney

STANDARD
PUBLISHING
Cincinnati, Ohio

Thorne Twins Adventure Books

Jaws of Terror
The House That Ate People
The Great UFO Chase
Secret of Pirates' Cave

Library of Congress Cataloging-in-Publication Data

Courtney, Dayle.
      The house that ate people / Dayle Courtney.
          p. cm. — (Thorne Twins adventure books)
      Summary: When a foreign dignitary is kidnapped during a
stay in New York City, twins Eric and Alison try to solve the
mystery of his disappearance.
      ISBN 0-87403-832-4
      [1. Mystery and detective stories. 2. Twins—Fiction. 3. New
York (N.Y.)—Fiction. 4. Christian life—Fiction.] I. Title. II.
Series: Courtney, Dayle. Thorne Twins adventure books.
PZ7.C83158Ho 1991
[Fic]—dc20   91-9685
                                                    CIP
                                                    AC

Revised copyright © 1991, The STANDARD PUBLISHING
      Company, Cincinnati, Ohio.
A division of STANDEX INTERNATIONAL Corporation.
Printed in U.S.A.

Contents

1 • *Mystery Marker*

The spiky skyscrapers of Manhattan loomed far below, highlighted by shafts of brilliant morning sunshine. Alison and Eric Thorne had visited some of the most beautiful and exciting places in the world, yet their pulses still beat a little faster as they looked down at the eye-filling spectacle of New York City.

Soon their 747 was touching down and taxiing to the gate.

"'Bye now," smiled the stewardess, as they filed out of the airliner with the other passengers.

"Why do you suppose they're keeping everything so secret?" Alison mused as they paused inside the terminal building to look around.

"Dunno," said Eric. "It's been like this ever since Dad got back from Hajar."

His sister grinned. "Maybe they're tapping us for secret agents!"

A tall, husky, gray-suited man strode toward them. "Eric and Alison Thorne?" he asked.

"Yes," smiled Alison.

"Well, you're certainly easy to identify!" He squeezed

Eric's hand in a muscular grip. "Not many sets of twins on a typical flight."

The relationship of the two teenagers was obvious at a glance, even though at sixteen Eric had sprouted a few inches taller than his sister. Lithe, bronzed, and athletic, with jet black hair and startling vivid eyes—Eric's sapphire blue, Alison's a deep darkling topaz—they were used to people turning their heads for a second look.

No doubt most people would have looked even harder had they known who the twins were supposed to meet while they were in New York.

"I'm Ed Bancroft, with the State Department," he said, showing them his credentials. "If you have no other bags to pick up, we'll be going out to my car. I'll fill you in there."

They each had only a flight bag, and Alison a smaller bag on a shoulder strap. Bancroft took Alison's flight bag and they walked to a lower level of the airport, to a small parking lot reserved for airport security. They got in a large silver-blue Chevy and minutes later, they were whizzing along a crowded expressway.

"Sorry to be so secretive about this whole deal," Bancroft began, "but this is the way they wanted to handle it. Ever hear of the Emir of Hajar?"

"Yes," Eric began. He was sitting in the front seat with Bancroft, and Alison leaned closer from the back seat. "Maybe we should tell you as much as we know. Our father works with the IAF, the International Agricultural Foundation, and he was visiting some of the Persian Gulf countries last month. He got to meet the Emir of Hajar at some sort of reception. They only talked for a minute, but he found out the Emir had a son our age."

Alison went on. "So he said something to the Emir like, 'we'd be glad to have him come and visit sometime,' you know, just being polite. He didn't think anything would come of it, but two weeks ago we got the letter from the

State Department asking if we could come here and meet the Emir's son."

"And also not to talk to anyone about it," added Eric. The car had just come out of a tunnel, and now they were driving across midtown Manhattan.

Ed Bancroft nodded. "We're trying to keep the Prince's visit out of the press entirely, as a security matter," he said. "Hajar is a tiny country, but it's the world's eleventh largest exporter of oil. The Emir—whose name, by the way, is Nasreddin Ibn al Azzam—is a very rich and powerful man. You might have read that he just bought an enormous ruby at an auction last week, for two million dollars. He's also just bought himself a mansion across the Hudson —or at least he's about to."

"You mean he's coming to live here?" asked Eric.

"Nope, just wants a little sixty-room shack to hang his turban in whenever he drops over for a shopping trip."

"Where do we come in on all this, Mr. Bancroft?" asked Alison.

"You already know the Emir has a son just about your age. His name is Haroun al Azzam. He wants to become Americanized, because later on he'll be coming over here to enter college. So his daddy, the Emir, decided it would be nice for Haroun to spend some time in a typical American home and meet some typical American teenagers."

Alison and Eric exchanged startled glances.

"He's coming to live with us in Illinois?" Eric blurted.

Ed Bancroft chuckled at the teens' expressions. "That's correct. For a few days."

"Well, when do we meet him?" asked Alison.

"At eleven o'clock, to be precise. Part of the security cover is that his royal jet will land at Newark Airport, where no one expects foreign celebrities to arrive. A helicopter will take him from there to Morristown Airport, where you two will meet him."

"Morristown?" asked Eric.

Bancroft nodded. "Morristown, New Jersey. Shouldn't take much more than an hour at this time of day."

"And what happens after we meet Prince Haroun?" said Alison. "I mean, how do we get from Morristown back to good old Ivy, Illinois?"

"Don't know." He shrugged. "And believe me, I'm leveling with you. It's all part of the tight security. No one's being told any more than he needs to know. I have the impression that you'll go from the airport to this mansion the Emir's buying—that is, if the prince hasn't already done so. But that's only a guess."

They had gone into another tunnel, and now they came out onto another maze of expressways. Soon, though, they were driving through a greener, more pleasant suburban landscape.

"As you know, there's always the threat of terrorists, and the Emir's rule in Hajar isn't all that stable, either. Some factions over there would like nothing better than to topple the Emir from his throne or even assassinate Prince Haroun while he's visiting here in the U.S.A.

"It was decided that the best security measure will be simply not to draw attention to Prince Haroun's presence in this country. The prince and his father, the Emir, want it that way. They want him to be exposed to the American way of life with no protective layers in between. Even back home in Ivy, you'll let on that he's just an ordinary exchange student. Neither you nor he will be guarded by the Secret Service or the FBI or any of our own security people."

He glanced over at Eric and Alison and grinned. "Not that we anticipate any trouble, of course. But normally we try to have some security people around to stay on top of things."

Eric and Alison glanced at each other, not sure whether to feel exhilarated or apprehensive.

It was not yet 11:00 when they pulled into the Morris-

10

town Airport parking lot. As soon as Mr Bancroft had braked to a halt, a tall, broad-shouldered young man strode to the car. He flashed his credentials before opening the car door for them.

"Agent Parker, FBI. How do you do, Mr. Thorne, Miss Thorne. Mr. Bancroft." He glanced at his watch. "The prince is due at eleven hundred hours. We have received word that his transportation has departed from Newark. Come with me, please—and bring your bags!"

The twins glanced at Ed Bancroft as Parker marched off ahead of them. Bancroft smiled faintly.

Parker led them toward a small group of cars parked at one end of the field near a hangar. Among them was a long black Lincoln Continental, so glossy it might just have been driven off the showroom floor—presumably the royal limousine.

"The car is bulletproof, and its driver will be the prince's personal manservant and bodyguard. He flew over here yesterday." He pointed out a huge, swarthy, hawk-nosed man with a fierce black mustache, wearing a *keffiyeh,* or Arab headdress and a uniform. "Highly trained in nearly every form of combat, I'm told, and ready to lay down his life for Prince Haroun."

"But the prince is still supposed to be just an ordinary exchange student?" Eric asked, with a touch of irony.

"Well . . . let's say a *wealthy* exchange student," Bancroft quipped. "With an Arab oil sheik for a daddy."

The chauffeur stood apart disdainfully from several other men, who broke off their chatting to be introduced to Eric and Alison. The rest included another State Department official, an oil company rep, and Mr. Mehmet Farouk, bearded and plump, who turned out to be Hajar's representative to the United States.

Eric wondered if there were a bunch of FBI agents lurking somewhere around the airport.

"Well, well!" Mr. Farouk beamed at the twins. "I can see

11

at once that two better companions could not have been chosen to show his Royal Highness the American way of life!"

When the introductions were over, Alison turned back to Agent Parker. "What exactly are the arrangements? I mean, for traveling back to Illinois with the prince?"

Eric grinned at his sister's question.

"Upon the prince's arrival," Parker replied, "you will accompany him to a mansion the Emir is buying. There you will meet Mr. Al Ghazali."

"Al Ghazali!" Eric exclaimed. "You mean the running back for the Chicago Bears?"

"Affirmative. You may not be aware that he's of Arab extraction. His parents immigrated to this country from Hajar after the second World War. Mr. Ghazali has agreed to act as purchasing agent in the sale of the mansion, so the real estate people don't even know yet that the real buyer is the Emir of Hajar. Once the prince has a chance to look at the mansion, Mr. Ghazali will close the deal and drive back with you to Illinois."

"Sounds great!" said Eric.

"It'll also give the prince a better chance to see the country," Alison added.

A rackety noise drew all eyes skyward. A whirlybird was approaching, which soon revealed itself as a big U.S. Air Force transport helicopter. It settled down ponderously on the airfield. As the welcoming group surged toward it, an American officer leaped out and saluted. Then Prince Haroun emerged.

He was shorter than Eric, about the same height as Alison, and stockily built. White teeth gleamed in a boyish grin, contrasting with his deeply tanned complexion. He was wearing a short-sleeved khaki safari jacket and pants to match.

He breezed through the introductions to the older group politely but quickly. When he turned to the Thorne twins, his attitude changed markedly. His onyx-dark eyes sparkled and his flow of remarks became more lively. It was obvious to all that he had been looking forward to this meeting with the two American teenagers.

"We shall get along famously, I am sure!" he told them. "I am looking forward with the keenest anticipation to seeing—how do you say in America?—your hometown?"

"We look forward to having you as our guest," Eric responded.

"And we hope you'll enjoy your stay," Alison added.

"There is not the slightest doubt but that I shall!" Haroun's smiling gaze swept over Alison's trim figure in a way that Eric didn't entirely approve of. Nor did he like the patronizing tone that crept into the prince's voice as he replied to the feminine member of the Thorne family.

"You will excuse me a moment, please," Haroun said to the group in general, "while I speak to one of the world's greatest fighting men—Captain Yusef Said!" (He pronounced the name *sah-EED*.)

A shy smile broke out on the mustached face of the chauffeur as the prince turned to him. Much to the twins' surprise, the gigantic Arab knelt and kissed the hand of his much younger and smaller royal master.

Haroun introduced him personally to Eric and Alison. "Yusef served in the Arab Legion and the Trucial Oman Scouts," he explained, "as well as in the elite British Parachute Regiment. There is no one whom my father and I trust more completely!"

It was the official delegation's turn to be surprised as the prince briskly waved Eric and Alison into his limousine, jumped in beside them, and with a quick command in Arabic, ordered Yusef to get going.

The Lincoln Continental's engine purred powerfully to life. "Cheers!" said the prince, waving impishly out the window. Alison smothered a giggle at the dumbfounded looks on the officials' faces as the limousine zoomed off.

"I think they were expecting a longer powwow," she murmured.

"*Powwow!* An American Indian word, is it not?" said the prince, looking delighted to hear it. "Yes, I do not doubt that it was rude of me to leave them so abruptly. But to tell the truth, these official . . . powwows . . . give me—how do you call it?—a pain in the neck." He chuckled and gazed out the window—almost greedily, it seemed, as if eager to drink in all the sights of this strange new country.

"This is your first visit to America?" Eric inquired.

"Yes, my very first! I have not seen very much of the world. I attended school in Switzerland, and I have accompanied my father on several journeys outside of Hajar, but this is the first time I feel like a genuine tourist. I cannot tell you what a thrill it will be to travel by car through so much of your great country!"

Eric smiled. "There's a lot of it to see. And right now we're going to see this mansion your father's buying?"

"Yes, that is correct," Haroun nodded. "I am to give it a final inspection on the Emir's behalf. If I like it, and Mr. Al Ghazali advises that it seems a wise choice, the purchase will be made immediately. Then we shall set out with him for your home in Illinois."

"How did your father happen to pick Mr. Ghazali?" said Alison. "He's not a professional real estate agent, is he?"

"Certainly not!" The prince's tone was scornful. "He is a military man, like Yusef, and one of the world's top athletes!"

"That's right. After college, he served in the Air Force as a fighter pilot," Eric remarked. "I'd forgotten."

"It is not forgotten in Hajar, I assure you!"

Haroun spoke about Al Ghazali as if the football star were a national idol in tiny Hajar. Apparently Ghazali was one of the best-known Americans in the Arab world. Even the prince himself seemed to regard the Bears' running back as a personal hero.

14

"And not only this," he added, "but we will all attend the Chicago Bears football match this Sunday as his guests!"

"All right!" said Eric. "That's with the Detroit Lions—it could help decide who goes to the Super Bowl!"

Haroun picked up the voice tube and spoke in Arabic to the chauffeur, who was separated by glass from the passenger compartment. "Yusef says it is no more than half an hour's drive from here," the prince reported.

Alison had been carrying a small bag on a shoulder strap. As she slid it down off her shoulder, Eric heard a slight gasp.

"'Smatter?" he asked, flicking her a questioning glance.

"This," Alison frowned. She turned one end of her bag toward him, so he could see what had been stuck on it. A round white tag made of leather or vinyl plastic, a little bigger than a half dollar. It was pierced with a straight pin, which in turn had been stuck into the fabric of Alison's shoulder bag.

Something had been drawn in red and black ink on the white patch. Eric detached the tag for a closer look, then handed it to Alison with a puzzled expression.

The drawing looked like a crude outline of an Oriental castle or mosque, with a minaret on each side and a central dome in between. Inside was a red skull and crossbones.

"No idea how it got on your bag?"

Alison shrugged. "There were people all around us when we got off the plane and came through the terminal. Any one of them could have stuck this on."

"May I see?" said Prince Haroun.

Alison, who was seated between the two boys, handed him the white patch.

Haroun studied it with a puzzled frown. "I do not understand."

"Someone stuck it on my bag when we flew into New York this morning."

Haroun looked at Alison quizzically. "You say 'someone.' You have no idea *who?*"

Alison shook her head.

"Hmm. Most interesting."

"The big question," Eric said, "is, what does it mean?"

"I'm not sure I want to hear the answer," said Alison.

But this mystery only seemed to heighten the excitement the twins felt. The gigantic Arab was a skillful driver, and the luxurious limo made the ride a pleasure. Bit by bit as they became better acquainted, the three teenagers relaxed, and their conversation became a lively chatter.

At last Yusef turned off a four-lane highway onto a narrow, tree-shaded rural road. This was hilly country and their route wound pleasantly up and down over a rocky, wooded slope.

When their destination finally came into view, the Thorne twins stared in sheer admiration and astonishment.

"Wow! Mansion's hardly the word for it!" said Eric. "It looks more like a palace!"

"Something out of *The Arabian Nights!*" breathed Alison.

"It is called *El Gezirah*—which in Arabic means 'The Island,'" Haroun explained. "It was built by a rich man named Murdo McKee. He would come here when he wished to feel himself cut off from the outside world."

A little shiver of excitement ran through Alison. On hearing the name *El Gezirah*, she dimly recalled reading about the mansion somewhere, or seeing it pictured in a magazine. An architect had called it "the most romantic house in America."

The spectacle was breathtaking. The entire front of the mansion was a shimmering expanse of tile—sea green, yellow, beige, pearly pink and maroon—pierced by a single Moorish arched gateway. At each corner stood a slender tower, topped by a pointed onion-shaped dome. In the center the roof rose in a swelling sky-blue curve. It looked as if some huge genie had magically transported it here from Baghdad or Casablanca!

But Alison gasped in dismay.

"Something wrong?" Eric asked. The limousine had just pulled to a halt on the curving driveway in front of the mansion.

"The outline of the house! Don't you see it?" Alison fished in her pocket and pulled out the mysterious patch that had been stuck on her shoulder bag.

Eric glanced at the crude drawing, then up again at the house, and gave a low whistle. "Hey! You're right!"

A minaret on each side and a dome in the middle! It was an outline of *El Gezirah* in black ink—with a red skull and crossbones inside it!

2 • Sneak Attack

Yusef had gotten out of the limousine. He opened the car door on Prince Haroun's side and stood back, saluting respectfully while the three young people climbed out.

Haroun showed the mysterious tag to the gigantic Arab chauffeur and explained how it had turned up on Alison's bag. "What do you make of it, Yusef?"

The chauffeur scowled, then shook his head slowly. He spoke in English, following his master's example. "I do not know, Your Highness. But I do not like the look of it either."

"One might take it as a warning of danger inside the house." Haroun's voice was calmly casual as he handed the tag back to Alison. "Fortunately we need not stop here very long, I think."

He certainly knows how to keep his cool, she thought with reluctant admiration. Despite the prince's smile, the twins noticed that Yusef's right hand had come to rest on the grip of the heavy revolver holstered at his side. This might not be the first time Haroun had been confronted with a threat of danger or violence.

Another car was parked on the drive—a white Cadillac.

Eric noticed the small sticker on the rear bumper from the rental agency. "Must be Al Ghazali's car," he remarked.

Prince Haroun nodded. "Undoubtedly he is waiting for us inside."

A gardener had been mowing the lawn of the magnificently landscaped grounds as they drove up. Seeing the group standing by the limousine, he shut off his tractor-mower and came up to speak to them.

"You folks lookin' for someone?" He was an elderly man in overalls, with a seamed, weather-beaten face. His manner was polite enough, but his scowling, squinting expression gave him a rather sinister appearance.

"Mr. Alfred Ghazali," said the prince. He gave the gardener an icy stare, designed to put him in his place and let him know that he had dared to address royalty.

The old man simply shifted his quid of tobacco and replied, "He the feller that come here to look the place over afore buyin' it?"

"Yes, that is the person I am referring to."

Eric smothered a smile as the gardener jerked a thumb toward the Moorish archway. "In there somewhere. May not be too easy to find, though. Mighty big place."

Squirting tobacco juice inches from the prince's right shoe, the gardener turned and headed back to his mower.

Yusef, with a face like a thundercloud at such disrespect for his royal master, looked ready to go after the old man and grab him by the scruff of the neck. But Haroun restrained his huge retainer with a flick of his hand. "It is not important. Let us go and see for ourselves."

A wrought iron gate, which swung across the archway, was standing open. As they passed through, Eric saw a metal crest or coat-of-arms affixed to the gate bars.

Inside was a flagged courtyard, with a fountain in the middle topped by nymphs and dolphins. Beyond lay a wide, shallow flight of marble steps leading up to the front door of the mansion.

Haroun mounted the steps first. Not bothering to use the ornate knocker or bell, he tried the door of the mansion. It opened to his push.

Alison felt her heart in her throat. Thinking of the red death's-head, suddenly she wasn't sure she wanted to set foot inside *El Gezirah*. But she followed the others into a vast tiled foyer. Yusef, with a murmured apology to his master, insisted on entering first, gun in hand.

Even at first glance, the magnificence was breathtaking. In other rooms opening off the foyer could be seen marble columns, sumptuous Persian carpets and inlaid parquet floors, a sweep of spiral staircase, lofty ceilings decorated with gilt and painted murals, Oriental vases, imposing statuary, masses of beautifully upholstered furniture. Some, but not all, of the furniture was draped in dust sheets.

Eric gave another low whistle and grinned. "Some layout!"

His words seemed to fall into a bottomless well of silence, faintly echoing as they faded.

A large oil portrait of a bushy-browed man with a handlebar mustache and muttonchop side whiskers frowned down at them from the wall of the foyer. A brass plate at the bottom of the frame identified him as Murdo McKee.

Haroun turned to his retainer. "Call for Mr. Ghazali."

Yusef took a deep breath and bellowed, *"Mister Ghazali!"*

The syllables echoed and reechoed through the spacious rooms all around them.

"Again," the prince ordered.

"MISTER GHAZALI!"

Seconds later, the mansion settled back into silence.

"Well. Obviously the house is too big for even Yusef's voice to carry everywhere," Haroun said, looking around. "I suppose we shall have to look for him."

The twins would have started off together, but Haroun intervened, proposing that he and Alison search the rooms to the right, while Eric and the chauffeur explore the left half of the mansion. Yusef protested that he was under orders from the Emir not to leave the prince unprotected for a moment. In the end, all four began drifting through the house in a loose group.

Alison was fascinated by the bewildering variety of furnishings. The original owner, Murdo McKee, seemed to have been a man of wide tastes—if "taste" was quite the word. Despite the mansion's outer look of an Oriental palace, inside every room had its own unique decor. Some were crammed with heavy, plush Victorian furniture, glass-fronted knickknack cases, and ornately carved wood paneling. In others were delicate chairs and chaises of the French Empire period, upholstered in striped satin, or glowing medieval wall tapestries and Renaissance museum pieces. Still others had fireplaces tiled in Moorish mosaic designs, Oriental divans and cushions, Indian brass ornaments and Chinese Buddhas. In the library, the books were guarded by a colorful pair of carved lions that looked as if they'd been salvaged from an old merry-go-round.

One thing none of the rooms contained, however, was Al Ghazali. Even though Yusef shouted his name every few moments, there was no reply.

Prince Haroun was becoming impatient. "Our man is obviously not here," he declared.

"What if something's happened to him?" Alison said in a small voice.

The prince shrugged. "It would take us hours to search every room thoroughly. I believe I was told there are fifty-three in all. Come! Let us make sure that oaf outside knows what he is talking about!"

Turning on his heel, Haroun headed back to the foyer. Yusef was dispatched to fetch the gardener.

"Are you quite sure Mr. Ghazali is still here?" the prince

demanded when the old man came waddling into the mansion.

"Sure, I'm sure. You seen his car standin' outside, didn't-cha?"

"Then why can we not find him?"

"Didn't look in the right place, prob'ly."

Haroun's face flushed with anger. But he controlled his temper and restrained his giant bodyguard from cuffing some manners into the gardener.

"What about the owner of this house, or the real estate agency that's selling it?" Eric spoke up. "Didn't anyone meet Mr. Ghazali when he arrived here?"

"Sure, Fred Jessup."

"He's the agent?"

"Yup. Works for Ludlow Realty, same as I do."

"Well, where is he?"

"Went back to town, I 'magine."

"He just left Mr. Ghazali here alone?"

"Yup. Customer prob'ly wanted time to look the place over. All I know is, I seen Mr. Jessup drive off in his car."

"How long ago was that?"

"Oh, 'bout an hour or two 'fore you folks showed up."

The twins and the prince exchanged baffled glances.

"Are the phones working?" Alison asked. She had seen several in the course of their wanderings about the mansion; the nearest was in one corner of the foyer.

"Yes, Ma'am."

Eric found a scrap of paper in a pocket of his jacket and wrote down the number as the gardener rattled it off.

Having suggested the idea, Alison was chosen to call the realtor. A secretary answered and put Jessup on the line. He seemed a bit confused on hearing a female voice.

"You're the party who's buying *El Gezirah?*" he asked.

"Actually there are four people here," said Alison. "One is the buyer's son. He expected Mr. Ghazali to meet us, but we can't find him."

"You can't find him?"

"That's right."

"He was there when I left," Jessup insisted plaintively. "He said he'd call me when he was ready to talk business."

"Well, he's not here now."

There was a pause before Jessup said, "Maybe he went off on an errand . . . or to get a bite to eat."

"No, his car's still parked outside. And the gardener tells us he never left the house."

A much longer pause followed.

"I'll be right over." Jessup's voice was sounding increasingly odd, and Alison noticed a quaver as he spoke these last words.

"I think that would be a very good idea," she said sharply, and hung up.

The group waited restlessly. Yusef made occasional forays into other parts of the house at his master's command, to try shouting again for the missing football star. None of his shouts brought any response. The gardener, meanwhile, still placidly munching his cud of tobacco, had gone back to his lawn mowing.

Fred Jessup, when he arrived, proved to be a sharp-eyed, tweed-jacketed, solid-citizen type in his late thirties, with crisp sandy hair and horn-rimmed glasses. He kept nervously fingering a pipe. "I'm sure Mr. Ghazali must be somewhere in the house," he ventured after clearing his throat. "Have you looked down in the basement?"

"Actually, no," said Eric with a hopeful glance at Haroun and Alison.

Barrel-vaulted and stone-pillared, the basement looked like a subterranean movie set for a Frankenstein or Dracula horror film. Alison half expected to see bats fluttering out of the cobwebbed corners. Because of the clutter and vast cavernous expanse, it was hard to see all four walls at the same time. The contents ranged from empty wine racks, to a furnace and boiler that looked huge enough to steam-power a battleship, to dusty piles of discarded furniture.

Al Ghazali, however, remained missing, even though they continued the search through the three upper floors of the mansion.

"I can't understand it," said Jessup, scratching his head and looking around helplessly.

"Can't you?" said Alison, fixing him with her dark amber gaze.

"Wh-what do you mean, Miss . . . uh . . ."

"Thorne. I mean you may not understand Mr. Ghazali's disappearance, as you keep telling us, but still I get the feeling you're not all that surprised."

Fred Jessup cleared his throat again. "Well, to tell the truth, this, uh . . . isn't the first unexpected thing that's happened since Mr. Ghazali arrived."

"Explain, please," the prince said crisply.

Jessup said that the missing football star had arrived soon after 9:00 and was about to be shown around the mansion when the telephone rang. "I answered it, and the caller asked to speak to Mr. Ghazali. That kind of surprised me, because I'd been told he was coming here all the way from Illinois, and I didn't see how anyone there would know where to reach him in New Jersey. In fact Mr. Ghazali looked kind of surprised himself. Anyhow, he took the call, and when he hung up he seemed a little embarrassed. Then he said he'd changed his mind."

"About what?"

"About me showing him through the house. He said he'd decided he could inspect it quicker by himself, if I didn't mind leaving him here alone for a while. Then he'd call me back and I could answer any questions he might have before we closed the sale."

Eric said, "So you went off and left him here alone?"

Jessup nodded. "That's right. I went back to the office in town. And heard nothing more till this young lady called."

"You have no idea what that phone call was about?"

The real estate agent hesitated. "Not really. I got the impression some emergency might've come up . . . that maybe whoever phoned had to see him in a hurry. So he wanted me out of the way. I figured his caller might come here after I left, or maybe Mr. Ghazali would slip out long enough to see the person."

Alison said, "Was Mr. Ghazali given the phone number of this house before he came here?"

"No, Ma'am—not so far as I know. If he'd wanted to get in touch to change our appointment time, or anything like that, he would have called Ludlow Realty. There's no one out here anyhow, except the gardener and a handyman now and then."

"Would the phone number be listed in any directory?" Eric asked.

"Don't see how it could be. The phones were just put back in service a week or so ago."

"Under what name?"

Fred Jessup frowned uncertainly. "I don't really know. The agency, I guess—Ludlow Realty."

Another baffled silence followed before Alison took up the questioning again.

"Mr. Jessup, that phone call Al Ghazali got may have been unexpected, but it wasn't really all that strange, was it? You still expected to hear from him, didn't you? And then you expected to come back here and close the deal for this mansion, right?"

"Well, yes—of course."

"Then why do I keep getting the impression that his disappearance doesn't surprise you all that much? I don't doubt the news came as a shock, and yet, when I called, you sounded like you were thinking, *Oh no, not again!* . . . You know, as if this were something you'd hoped wouldn't happen, but now it had happened."

Eric shot an astonished glance at his sister. Alison had

a knack for putting herself in other people's shoes and understanding their feelings or reactions in awkward situations. But surely this was carrying the idea of "feminine intuition" a bit far!

Jessup, however, was looking highly uncomfortable—as if her guess had hit the mark. He blinked, took off his glasses, and polished them busily before replying.

"Miss Thorne, I don't know exactly how to say this, but . . . the fact is, Mr. Ghazali isn't the first person who's disappeared in this house."

"What?" Eric blurted, and the others looked equally dumbfounded.

"I think, Mr. Jessup," Prince Haroun said firmly, "you had better tell us exactly what you mean."

Fred Jessup started to reply, then gulped and seemed to swallow whatever he'd been about to say. "Sorry, sir, but I think I'd better let my boss, Mrs. Ludlow, do any explaining there is to be done."

"And where are we to find Mrs. Ludlow?"

"At our office in town." Jessup took a card from his wallet and gave brief directions.

"Very well." Prince Haroun took charge of the situation in royally decisive fashion. "Mr. Jessup, you will remain here, please, and continue to search for my father's agent, Mr. Ghazali. If you discover any indication of what has happened to him, kindly telephone your office at once. In the meantime, we shall proceed there and confer with your employer."

Minutes later, the big sleek Lincoln Continental limousine went purring down the horseshoe drive that curved in front of the mansion.

"How do people disappear *inside* houses?" Eric demanded of no one in particular.

"Good question," said Alison, "But it looks like we've just seen it happen. Or at least we've just *discovered* a case of it happening."

"Al Ghazali is a very big man," said Haroun. "Also very strong and tough and used to violence. It would certainly not be easy to *make* him disappear."

"You can say that again!" Eric agreed, thinking of the times he had seen the Bears' star running back smash his way through opposing linemen like a tank on two legs.

Their route took them back along the way they had come. By now their limousine had gone several miles from the mansion. The stretch of road they were following led downhill through a wooded gorge.

Their driver slowed. Ahead, the three teenagers could see a roadblock and a policeman waving a red flag, signaling them to stop. Behind him, two construction workers were digging up the road.

"What's going on?" Eric wondered aloud, but before he could finish his question he was thrown forward as Yusef slammed on the brakes. Before the limousine screeched to a halt, the huge Arab driver was slewing the wheel around and stepping on the gas again. Next moment the car was leaping across the shoulder of the road and arrowing its way at high speed through the trees and underbrush!

Behind them, the twins could hear angry shouts, then a volley of gunshots!

3 • Vanishing Victims

"They're shooting at us!" Alison exclaimed incredulously.

"So it seems." Prince Haroun's teeth gleamed in a grin of amusement—almost, Eric thought, as if he were enjoying himself.

Despite the Lincoln's long wheelbase and splendidly engineered suspension, the three were jouncing around wildly as the car plunged up the rugged incline.

"Where are we going?" Eric asked as clearly as he could under such jolting, juddering circumstances.

"Away from the gunfire, I trust!" said Haroun.

"But where *to?*"

"Ah, I leave that to Yusef's good judgment. Rest assured, he will have traveled this road at least two times in order to inspect it thoroughly before picking me up at the airport this morning. That is his usual security procedure. Also," the prince added, "he will have acquainted himself with every side road intersecting the route."

Ten minutes elapsed before the limousine came out of the woods onto a dirt road. It seemed nothing short of a miracle that the car's springs were still unbroken. Eric decided that Yusef must have some sixth sense that enabled him to thread his way so expertly over such an obstacle course—avoiding trees, brush, rocks, hillocks, and gullies—while at the same time nosing out the shortest route to the nearest road.

The giant Arab finally pulled onto a clear stretch of shoulder just before the dirt road joined a blacktop highway. After a glance over his shoulder into the passenger compartment, he got out of the car to inspect its condition. So did the three young people.

"How did you know we were going to be shot at, Captain Said?" Eric asked the chauffeur.

"On our way here, I noticed no area in need of repair." The mustached driver shrugged. "It was a perfect spot for an ambush—and that roadblock ruse is an old trick. After a while, one gets to *know* such things—the same way a hunter and his prey learn to sense each other's moves."

"Now wait a minute!" Alison burst out indignantly, glaring at the three males. "You talk as if there's nothing unusual about riding into death traps! Those men were shooting *guns* at us back there—probably trying to *kill* us!"

"Trying to kill *me,* more likely," Haroun corrected her. "Or, let us say, me and my bodyguard. You two had the bad luck to be riding in the same car with me."

"What difference does that make?" Alison retorted scornfully. "The point is, nobody's supposed to go around gunning people down on nice quiet country roads—not you or us or anyone else!"

"But, alas, someone just did. Or tried to."

"Exactly! So let's not take it quite so calmly—as if it were no more serious than a flat tire. That looks like a telephone tucked into the back of the front seat—right?"

Prince Haroun acknowledged that the item in question was indeed a mobile telephone.

"Then why aren't you on it, reporting the attack to the police or the FBI or somebody?"

"Because, my dear Miss Thorne," the prince regarded her with a patronizing smile that infuriated Alison, "I have no intention of letting my visit to your fascinating country be cut short or spoiled. But that is exactly what would happen if any of those agencies were informed of this attempt on my life."

"One of those agencies could *save* your life if there's another attempt," Alison pointed out.

"I feel perfectly safe, thank you, with Captain Yusef Said to guard me. You have just seen how efficiently he does so." The young prince beamed at his bodyguard.

But the gigantic chauffeur looked uncomfortable. "Your Highness," he rumbled, "there may be a certain wisdom in what the young lady says."

"Are you afraid you may not be able to perform your duties well enough to protect me from harm, Yusef?" barked Prince Haroun.

The huge Arab drew himself stiffly to attention with a look of outraged military virtue. "Certainly not, Your Highness!"

"Nor am I. So let us say no more about it. As for you"—Haroun turned to the Thorne twins with a boyish, conspiratorial smile—"I forbid you both even to mention the subject to anyone else without my express permission. May I have your word on that?" He looked from one to the other.

Now it was Eric's turn to squirm uncomfortably, especially when his gaze met Alison's. Despite the shock of being fired on, he felt a bit infected by Prince Haroun's high-spirited reaction—as if dangerous adventures like this were what kept life interesting.

On the other hand, not only his own safety but Alison's was involved. And Prince Haroun's safety as well. He and Alison both would have to admit that the prince's safety was more important than an interesting adventure.

Eric took a deep breath.

"Look, Prince Haroun. Alison and I are as eager as you

are to enjoy your royal visit. But part of our duty as host and hostess is to see that you're safe."

"I have already told you, Friend Eric, that I feel perfectly safe with Yusef to guard me."

"Of course. And he's just proved that he's doing a great job. But we were told that our government's people wanted more security to protect you too. They only agreed to the present arrangements because your father, the Emir, wanted it that way."

"Very well!" Haroun smiled charmingly at the twins. "If I inform the Emir of what has happened, and he says we may still proceed without a retinue of your policemen and FBI agents to guard us, will you accept his decision?"

Eric and Alison exchanged glances again.

"OK, you've got a deal," said Eric.

"Splendid!" Haroun seized Eric's hand and pumped it. Then, as Alison blushed (whether from pleasure or embarrassment, Eric wasn't sure), he raised her slender hand to his lips, like a fairy-tale Prince Charming. "And now, since the car seems hardly scratched," he added, "let us be off again!"

The twins introduced Prince Haroun and his bodyguard to the pleasures of American hamburgers, french fries, and milkshakes at a roadside diner. More than an hour later, they arrived at the real estate office in the nearby town of Verdon. They hoped to be told that Al Ghazali had returned from wherever he'd disappeared to.

Mrs. Grace Ludlow, the owner/manager of Ludlow Realty, was a large woman, sharp-faced but hearty in manner, with blue-rinsed hair and rimless glasses pinched on a small bird beak of a nose.

"Let me get this straight. You're the buyer's son?" she inquired, peering intently at the prince.

Haroun smiled back blandly. "My father, Mr. Azzam, is, let us say, the head of the firm that is purchasing *El Gezirah*. Mr. Ghazali was to act as his adviser and agent.

But he seems to have disappeared. Unless, that is, he has been found since we left the house?"

Eric and Alison looked hopefully at the lady realtor, but Mrs. Ludlow dashed their hopes with a shake of her head.

"Sorry, Fred Jessup hasn't seen hide nor hair of him. I talked to Fred twice on the phone before you got here."

"Mr. Jessup," said Alison, "told us this wasn't the first case of someone disappearing from *El Gezirah*."

"Hmph. Well now, I wouldn't attach too much significance to that."

"Maybe you'd care to tell us exactly what he meant," Alison persisted politely but firmly.

"What did you say your name was, dear?" Mrs. Ludlow's gaze through her pince-nez glasses became a trifle beady-eyed.

"Alison Thorne. My brother and I are friends of the Azzam family."

"Indeed? How very interesting. Well, dear, it's true. There's been a certain amount of gossip about people getting lost in that mansion. But then *El Gezirah's* an immense place, isn't it? Fifty-three rooms. I'm sure you can see how easy it would be to lose your way inside it, or how long it would take to look through the whole house, room by room. Perhaps Mr. Ghazali simply fell asleep."

Prince Haroun's gaze became even steelier than the lady realtor's. "Mr. Ghazali knew that we were to arrive before noon, Madame. It is now almost two o'clock. I cannot believe that he would fail to appear or let us know his whereabouts, if he were safe and sound."

Mrs. Ludlow hemmed and hawed, twiddled her fingers on her desk top, and shrugged her massive shoulders. "I really don't know what to tell you. I've never even met this Mr. Ghazali. We were simply told by your father's representatives in New York that he would be coming here this morning to inspect the house and give his final approval of the purchase. What more can I say?"

"Perhaps we should notify the police," said Alison.

Fearing this might provoke a response from Haroun that would give away his royal identity, Eric broke in. "Who exactly owns the mansion?"

"The McKee estate," said Mrs. Ludlow. "That is, the present-day heirs of Murdo McKee, who originally built the house. It passed first to his son. Then later on, the State of New Jersey took charge and opened it to the public as an historical museum. But now his heirs have decided to sell it, and my agency was asked to handle the transaction."

"When you say your agency was asked, I assume that means someone connected with the estate did the asking?" Alison said.

"You assume correctly, dear."

"And who would that be?"

"The chief executor."

Eric kept his lips from twitching in a smile. "Would you care to tell us his name, Mrs. Ludlow?"

The lady realtor glanced irritably from Eric to Prince Haroun. "Do you wish to get in touch with him, Mr.—uh, Azzam?"

"Naturally. Since you are unable to give us any details about previous cases of people disappearing from *El Gezirah,* perhaps he can do so."

Mrs. Ludlow pursed her lips, wrote a name and address on a note pad, then tore off the slip of paper, and without a word handed it across the desk to Haroun.

"One other question, Mrs. Ludlow," said Eric. "I'm sure you'll understand why it's necessary to ask, so you won't take offense. Are Mr. Jessup and the gardener absolutely trustworthy?"

"Young man, if I didn't trust Fred Jessup, I wouldn't employ him as a salesman. As for the gardener, Tom Appleton, he's been tending the grounds of *El Gezirah* ever since I can remember."

The three felt sure Mrs. Ludlow was watching them through her office window as they climbed back into the prince's limousine, parked on the street outside.

"Well? What would you suggest we do now?" Haroun asked the twins. "See this lawyer fellow?" He showed them the slip of paper, on which Mrs. Ludlow had written:

G. Humphrey Ward, attorney
Danforth, Ward & Milgrim

Below the name of the law firm were a phone number and address in Newark.

"Seems like a reasonable move," Eric agreed.

Alison suggested they call first to make sure the lawyer would be in his office. Haroun did so, and presently they were rolling eastward through the autumn countryside, aflame with the scarlet and gold of crisping leaves.

Thirty-five minutes later, Yusef deposited them outside an office building in downtown Newark. Ten floors up, a secretary ushered them into Mr. Ward's office.

A gaunt, elderly man with a few strands of thinning gray hair brushed carefully across his bald dome, the lawyer eyed Prince Haroun shrewdly as they were introduced. But if he had placed Haroun as the son of the Emir of Hajar, he gave no sign. G. Humphrey Ward was clearly a man of discretion.

"You wish to know first, I assume," he began when they were all seated, "about your missing friend, Mr. Ghazali. I am sorry to say that, up until five minutes ago anyway, there was still no word of what has happened to him. Mr. Jessup, however, is continuing to search the house thoroughly with the help of Mrs. Ludlow and another member of her real estate firm, as well as the gardener."

"I imagine she also told you we were interested in finding out about other cases of people disappearing from that house," Eric said.

Mr. Ward nodded unhappily. "It's true such disappearances have occurred. Mind you, I don't wish to give the impression there is anything—er, *dangerous* about the McKee mansion. I mean, such as a hole that people fall into and break their necks and are never heard from again. I'm sure there's a perfectly simple explanation of each case. Still"—he spread his hands in a vague shrug of puzzlement—"they have occurred."

Alison gave him a smile of encouragement. "Perhaps you'd be kind enough to tell us about them."

"Hmm, well . . . I daresay I might run over them briefly. The first such case involved Mr. Murdo McKee himself."

"The man who built the mansion?"

"Yes. He was living there alone at the time, with just his servants. He carried on a number of business enterprises from his office here in Newark—manufacturing, coal mining, shipping, zinc smelting, and so on. On this particular occasion, some sort of business trouble had arisen. A number of people wanted to get hold of him—including certain of his own employees and associates as well as other businessmen. But his servants insisted that he wasn't home—that he must have gone out late the night before and hadn't returned."

"What happened?" Eric asked.

Mr. Ward shrugged again. "He couldn't be found. Yet about ten days later, after the crisis had blown over, he turned up unharmed. A servant found him sound asleep in bed one morning, as if nothing out of the ordinary had happened."

"*Bismillah!*" Prince Haroun exclaimed, frowning. "How can this be?"

"You may well ask, sir. Mr. McKee himself offered no explanation. He simply said he had no memory of those missing days. After that, one or two other cases occurred. On one occasion, a servant vanished. Another time it was a workman or carpenter—I'm not quite sure which—who was doing some painting or plastering or repair work in the house."

Alison said, "Were they ever found?"

"Oh yes, after several days. Both cases occurred at times when Mr. McKee was away on business trips. They caused quite a fuss. I believe the workman's boss even insisted the police get a search warrant and go through the house, room by room."

"With no results?"

"None whatever. They found no trace of either missing man. However, in both cases, the workman and the servant each reappeared soon after Mr. McKee returned home."

Alison frowned. "How do you mean, 'reappeared'?"

The elderly lawyer snapped his fingers. "Just like that. They were suddenly seen in the house again, acting as if nothing unusual had happened. Both insisted they had no recollection of those missing days."

"Those were the only cases?"

Mr. Ward sighed. "Well . . . no. After Mr. McKee died, his son Stuart took over the house. Both of them were harsh-tempered, dictatorial men—hard to get along with. At any rate, they never got along with each other. And it was Stuart McKee's daughter—that is, the old man's granddaughter—who became the next person to vanish from *El Gezirah*."

Prince Haroun was listening in wide-eyed fascination. "It sounds like a tale from the *Thousand and One Nights!*"

"Quite so. The young lady, Miss Fiona McKee, was only eighteen at the time."

"Did her father report her missing?" Alison inquired.

"By no means. Shortly before she vanished, she had become engaged to a young man named Jared Custer. Her father strongly disapproved. When she failed to appear in church for her wedding, her fiance came storming up to the mansion, demanding that her father release her. Custer assumed she was being held prisoner, to prevent the marriage. Her father slammed the door in his face, whereupon Custer too went to the police and had the mansion searched."

"Was she found?"

G. Humphrey Ward shook his balding head gloomily. "No. As far as I know, she never did turn up. And I believe there may have been—hmph—one or two other unpleasant, unexplained incidents while Stuart McKee was occupying the house."

"Mrs. Ludlow mentioned that *El Gezirah* became a museum for a while," put in Eric.

"Er, yes, that is so."

"Then how come it was put up for sale?"

The lawyer cleared his throat, looking as if he wished Mrs. Ludlow had kept her big mouth shut. "Well, you see, mansions of that size are rather expensive to own, because of taxes and upkeep. After Mr. Stuart McKee passed on, *El Gezirah* was inherited by another relative, who considered it a white elephant. So he arranged to turn it over to the State of New Jersey, to be operated as an historical museum. Both the architecture and furnishings, of course, are quite remarkable, making the house a genuine historical art treasure."

"All the more reason for keeping it open to the public," said Eric.

"Yes, quite so. Unfortunately, several visitors to the museum also disappeared. And some local newspaperman wrote a series of feature articles about the mansion—stories depicting *El Gezirah* as a spooky old ruin, full of booby traps. Luridly sensational stuff, designed to inspire scare headlines. As if the rooms weren't even safe to walk through. He stirred up such a tempest in a teapot, the house was finally closed to the public."

Prince Haroun gave the lawyer a quizzical frown. "Are you saying *El Gezirah* is still a museum, even though it is now being offered for sale?"

"No, no—not at all, sir! In fact that is precisely why the house is being offered for sale. One of the clauses in the agreement, you see, stated that if New Jersey failed to maintain the house as a museum, it would automatically revert to the McKee Estate. The present heir pounced on that clause, insisted on taking possession again, and had the house put up for sale."

A tall grandfather clock stood in one corner of the elderly lawyer's office. The three teenagers could hear it ticking sedately in the silence that followed his strange story.

"There must be some rational explanation for all those disappearances," Alison murmured thoughtfully.

"Of course there is, my dear."

Eric said, "Didn't the state government try to find one, after the museum was closed?"

"Oh, there was talk of appointing a commission to investigate—consisting of an architect and engineer and a few other so-called experts. But talk was all it amounted to. Nothing ever got done. So finally the present McKee heir reclaimed the mansion and ordered it put up for sale."

"Assuming we wanted to do something," said Alison, "where would be the best place to find out the details of those other disappearances?"

"Well . . . hmm, let me see." Mr. Ward toyed with his desk pen for a few moments, then set it down and fingered a heavy silver cigar lighter. "You could always go to the offices of the Newark *Record* and look up those old newspaper articles I mentioned. When all's said and done, I suppose they do provide the most complete history of *El Gezirah*."

The lawyer's frosty eyebrows lifted in a glance at his three visitors. "The publisher of the *Record* happens to be a friend of mine," said Mr. Ward, reaching for the telephone. "Why don't I call him and arrange for you folks to read through those old feature stories. . . ."

Had the shrewd old lawyer simply proposed the newspaper research as a way to maneuver them out of his office? Possibly so, the teenagers decided, once they were back in the royal limousine.

Still, both Eric and Alison wanted to follow through. It certainly didn't seem as if notifying the police would bring Al Ghazali back any sooner, even if Prince Haroun *had* been willing to face the blaze of publicity that was bound to result. The police hadn't been able to find any of the mansion's previous victims, so why expect them to find Al?

Meanwhile, the prince phoned his country's U.N. representative in New York—Mr. Mehmet Farouk, whom the twins had met at the airport. As a result of this call, it was decided that Yusef would drop Eric and Alison at the newspaper office, then drive Haroun to the United Nations, across the Hudson River in Manhattan, and return to pick up the twins in Newark at 5:30.

A uniformed guard in the lobby of the *Record* building directed the Thornes to the newspaper's morgue and reference library on the third floor. It was a room crammed to the ceiling with shelves of bound volumes of newspapers from recent years, row upon row of file cabinets, books and encyclopedias of every description, and several microfilm and microfiche readers in a corner cubbyhole for checking out older issues of the paper.

A helpful but overworked librarian gave the twins the bound volumes of the *Record* for the years and months in question, and they settled down for a spell of intensive reading.

Alison nudged her brother after one glance at the first feature story on the McKee mansion. It was titled:

THE HOUSE THAT EATS PEOPLE!

4 • The Man With the Eyepatch

Eric chuckled as he read the words Alison was pointing out. "Great title!"

All the same, the mental image of the missing football star getting gobbled up by that weird Oriental mansion gave him a nervous twinge in the pit of his stomach. His mind was soon occupied by other thoughts, however, as he scanned the columns of newsprint.

Soon after the mansion had been opened to the public, they learned, a visitor to the museum had disappeared. He turned up months later, under bizarre circumstances, unable to give a clear account of what had happened to him.

His disappearance had inspired a *Record* reporter named Tom Peel to write a series of feature stories on the strange history of *El Gezirah*. Peel's sensational yarn-spinning apparently had aroused avid interest among readers, resulting in a flood of letters to the editor.

About six weeks later, another person disappeared inside the mansion, unleashing another spate of letters and phone calls from readers.

Several other mysterious disappearances followed,

spaced over the next two or three years. Each time, Peel had gone to town on the story, following up with a day-by-day report on the search for the missing victim, which whetted public interest to a keen pitch. His original feature series on the history of *El Gezirah* was also reprinted, slightly updated for each new case.

The last disappearance had caused such an explosive public uproar that the governor of New Jersey finally ordered the mansion closed in the interest of public safety, until a commission could be appointed to find out what had happened to the vanished victims.

By then, even that old monster of local folklore, the Jersey Devil, was being dragged out of mothballs to explain their fate.

In fact, none of the house's recent victims had ever been found. Other pressing political problems had come up to delay the appointment of the much talked-about "investigation commission." Meanwhile, the heir of old Murdo McKee had snatched the mansion back from the state and put it on the real estate market, for sale to any multimillionaire who happened to be shopping for a really eye-catching rural retreat.

And now, it seemed, *El Gezirah* had claimed another victim!

"Well? What do you make of it all?" Eric asked Alison, closing up the last bound volume. As usual, she had finished first.

Her dark amber eyes were thoughtful as she shook her head in bewilderment. "The whole thing seems unbelievable, doesn't it?"

A fiendish look came over Eric's face. "Just imagine the bodies of all those victims moldering away, somewhere inside the sinister old McKee mansion!" he wrung his hands gloatingly. "Probably mummified by now!"

"Ugh! Stop it! Don't even *say* such things!" Alison flared back.

Eric saw the librarian glancing at them sharply and lowered his voice. "Seriously. What's our next move?"

"Well . . . these articles are all very interesting, but they really haven't told us much."

"You can say that again!"

"On the other hand, the reporter who wrote them, Tom Peel, must know more about that house and what's happened in it than any other person alive."

A photo feature in one issue included a few shots of the author himself. They showed him standing in front of *El Gezirah* or pointing out some of the more colorful aspects of its interior. Alison reopened one of the bound volumes of newspapers, leafed through its pages again to one of the articles, and pointed the reporter out to her brother. "Looks like a dashing foreign correspondent," Eric commented.

Judging by his photograph, Peel was still in his early thirties—a tall, handsome man with a mop of dark hair and a pirate's patch over his left eye.

Alison said, "Think he might be able to offer any clues?"

"Hey, that's an idea! If we can keep him from getting too snoopy about why we're interested."

"Come on. Let's ask the librarian where to find him."

They carried the newspaper volumes back to her desk, and Alison pointed out the reporter's picture to her.

"Tom Peel?" The librarian frowned. "I'm afraid he doesn't work for the *Record* any more. As I recall, he left a couple of years ago—not long after the last of those feature stories, in fact."

"Is there anyone in the building who could tell us how to get in touch with him?" Eric asked.

"Hmm, let me see. I suppose Personnel might know, but I doubt if they'd give out his address or phone number. Of course, his editor might still know where to reach him."

"Could you tell us where to find his editor, then?"

"That would be Mr. Finburn. Go two floors up, through

the newsroom. You'll find his office in a corridor on the other side."

"Thank you very much," Eric said.

Getting out on the fifth floor, they made their way through a crowded newsroom where shirt-sleeved reporters and rewrite people talked on phones or typed on their computer keyboards, staring at the monitors. In a corridor beyond, after deftly evading a couple of harried secretaries, they found the glassed-in office of the managing editor.

They knocked and were told to come in. Mr. Finburn was built like a bull. His close-cropped thatch of curly grey hair looked like a skullcap coming unraveled.

"Yeah?"

"Uh, I'm Eric Thorne and this is my sister Alison, Mr. Finburn."

He stared at them nearsightedly, then perched a pair of spectacles on his nose for a better look.

"And what can I do for you?"

"We'd like to see one of your reporters, Tom Peel," said Alison.

"Tom's no longer working here. He did a series of feature stories a while back that stirred up a lot of interest and got him a couple of outside job offers. He wound up moving to New York to write books and magazine articles."

"Can you tell us how to get in touch with him?"

"Why do you want to know?"

Alison couldn't think of what to say, so Eric broke in. "We're, uh, doing some research on that old mansion that Mr. Peel wrote about. We just spent over an hour going through all his old feature articles about it, and we have some more questions."

"Mmph." Finburn flicked through the personal directory on his desk, then wrote down a phone number and address on a slip of paper, which he handed to Alison. "He lives in Queens. I can't guarantee you'll reach him. Tom had an accident recently, almost got run down by a truck. Nothing too serious, but he did get hit and had to go to the hospital for a few days. I haven't been able to get hold of him since, so he may have gone off somewhere to recuperate."

Alison rewarded the managing editor with a dazzling smile. A smile that made him beam back and sit up a little straighter, as if he had just shed a few years of age.

"Thanks, Mr. Finburn. You've been a great help."

He smiled back. "My pleasure, Miss Thorne."

They were on their way out through the ground-floor lobby when a security guard stopped them.

"Your name Thorne?"

"That's right."

It was the same guard who had directed them to the reference library when they first arrived in the *Record* building. He gave Eric an envelope that was hand-lettered in black ink:

ERIC & ALISON THORNE
(Now looking up back copies of the paper)

"Where'd this come from?" Eric asked the guard.

"Some kid walked into the lobby a couple of minutes ago and handed it to me. He just looked like a kid off the street. I suppose someone paid him to deliver it."

"OK, thanks."

People were milling about as the afternoon wore down to the close of another working day. The twins found a corner of the lobby where they were out of the stream of traffic, and Eric opened the envelope.

Inside was a crude cartoon. It showed a man with a black eyepatch stepping in front of a speeding truck. Underneath were a letter and number: U 2.

Eric gave one of his low whistles. "Tom Peel?"

"Who else," said Alison. "In other words, *we* could get run down by a truck too—if we try to find out why people disappear in the McKee mansion!"

"Are you saying we should quit right now?"

"No—just that someone wants us to."

They looked at each other in silence.

"Well?" Eric challenged.

"Well, nothing," said Alison. "We're both going to keep right on trying, so let's not waste time discussing *that* question. But we'd better face the fact that this could get dangerous."

"It already has."

"True, but this is the first time we've been threatened personally and warned to back off," she said, pointing to their names on the envelope.

Eric nodded thoughtfully. "How do you suppose whoever wrote this knew we'd come here to the *Record* building—and why?"

"I'd say that's the key question," Alison replied. "Unfortunately I don't know the answer."

Minutes later, through the glass doors of the lobby, they saw the royal limousine pull up to the curb outside. They hurried out and climbed in beside Prince Haroun.

The jaunty young Arab greeted them with a white-toothed smile. "Good news! Our United Nations representative, Mr. Farouk, called the palace in Hajar, and my father has given permission for me to stay here in New York for the present time."

"Did you tell him what happened?" asked Alison.

"As much as he needed to know. I said that Al Ghazali has become lost or delayed somewhere, so we must wait until he appears."

Eric said, "What about that roadblock ambush?"

Haroun shrugged and fluttered his hands vaguely. "The Emir is a man with grave responsibilities. I saw no point in worrying him needlessly."

The twins disapproved, though it was hard to frown at the prince when he flashed his infectious boyish grin.

"So what happens now?" said Eric.

"I shall be staying at the Stuyvesant Plaza Hotel in Manhattan, and a suite has been reserved for you and your sister too as my guests."

"Wow!" Eric and Alison exchanged glances again. There was no point in pretending the prospect didn't sound attractive.

"You will accept, of course?" Haroun added anxiously.

Alison smiled. "Thank you, Your Highness. We'd both like that. Since we came here to escort you home with us to Illinois, we'll certainly wait till you're ready to go—so I guess what you suggest is the most sensible thing to do."

"Right!" Eric chimed in enthusiastically, wishing he could made graceful speeches as easily as Alison.

"In the meantime," she went on, "may we use your car telephone to call *our* father and let him know?"

"By all means, please do!" said Haroun. "But on one condition."

Alison stopped short as she was about to reach for the mobile phone. "What's that?"

"That there be no more of this 'Your Highness' nonsense. From now on, you must call me Haroun, and I shall call you Alison and Eric."

The twins smiled and shook hands with him simultaneously.

"You've got a deal, Haroun," said Eric.

Besides being a consultant for the International Agricultural Foundation, the twins' father, Dr. Randall Thorne, was a professor of agronomy at Midwest University. He was often on leave of absence working for the Foundation, but this fall Dr. Thorne was on campus, teaching a full schedule of classes.

"How nice of the prince to provide you with a suite in such a luxury hotel!" he remarked, after hearing where the twins were to stay. "And don't worry about not getting home as soon as expected. At least I'll know you're in safe company."

Alison was a little annoyed with herself, however, to realize that she hadn't told him much more than Haroun had told *his* father. But, after all, what was the sense in worrying Dad needlessly?

She turned the phone over to Eric so he could talk to their father. He chatted briefly and then hung up.

"Now then," said Prince Haroun, "suppose you tell me all you have learned about the mysterious past history of *El Gezirah.*"

"Well," Alison replied. "It's a long story."

Just then Yusef's voice came over the speaking tube from the driver's compartment:

"Begging your pardon, Your Highness, but we are being followed!"

5 • A Weird Message

Haroun calmly picked up the mouthpiece of the tube. "Which car, Yusef?"

"A maroon Pontiac. But if Your Highness will permit a suggestion—perhaps it would be best not to look. This might betray our awareness of being followed, and thus put our pursuer on guard."

"Wise counsel, Yusef. I shall heed your advice. How long has the car been following us?"

"I noticed it only after we picked up your two friends at the newspaper building. Since then, it has been swerving in and out of traffic—apparently trying to keep us in sight. Possibly it has been trailing us much longer than that."

The late afternoon rush hour had arrived. They were now whizzing along a crowded, three-lane expressway that curved down to the mouth of the Lincoln Tunnel. As they approached the toll booths, the three lanes merged haphazardly with traffic from a lower-level expressway. Farther on, the cars split up again to enter the two separate passages that were now green-lighted to carry the eastbound flow into New York.

"We have eluded the Pontiac, I think," Yusef reported.

"It was edged aside into the other tunnel entrance." He kept a sharp lookout when they emerged into the streets of Manhattan minutes later. No maroon car was in sight.

"Excellent!" said Haroun, settling back comfortably. "Perhaps it was not following us after all."

Neither Eric nor Alison was about to jump to such a comforting conclusion. They thought it more likely that traffic was just more clogged in the other tunnel, preventing the Pontiac from catching up with them. Still, that was a stroke of luck if they *were* being shadowed by some enemy.

Meanwhile, both the prince and the twins observed the street scenes all about them with keen interest. If none too clean, New York City was certainly picturesque! Dingy brownstones and tenements, shops with window signs in Spanish and English, graceful but grimy turn-of-the-century townhouses—all huddling together in the shadow of glittering modern skyscrapers. Traffic crawled bumper-to-bumper, bottlenecked by double-parked delivery trucks and vans. People of every race, color, and description, dressed in styles ranging from the latest "in" fashions to the filthiest castoffs, were crowding every street corner.

"Why must everyone rush about so quickly?" Haroun wondered aloud.

"I'm not sure they know, either," said Eric.

Yusef bored his way crosstown, then turned left on Park Avenue, heading for the swank Upper East Side. The limousine had barely pulled up to the curb when the Stuyvesant Plaza doorman came rushing out from under the hotel's awning to open the door of the passenger compartment.

The three young people stepped out. Prince Haroun pressed a ten-dollar bill into the doorman's palm, not even noticing the size of the tip he was bestowing.

Another man hastened to accost them as they entered the hotel lobby—this one tall, thin, and sallow-skinned, with liquid dark eyes and a black mustache. He turned out to be a member of Hajar's United Nations delegation named Abu Kassim, who had been assigned to attend the needs of the royal visitor.

"Your Highness's guests have been given Suite 2407, just across the hall from your own," he announced. "A dinner table had been reserved for six forty-five o'clock in the hotel's Knickerbocker Club dining room, and here are the theater tickets Your Highness requested. I was also told to remind you that your Highness will be staying here incognito—registered under the name of Haroun Habib."

"Splendid, Kassim!" Prince Haroun slapped the diplomatic aide on the shoulder. He turned to the Thorne twins and gestured toward a bank of elevators. "Come! Let us see if our accommodations are suitable!"

They were not only suitable, they were palatial. A spacious, high-ceilinged sitting room in the middle of their suite—entered via an only slightly less spacious vestibule—with a luxurious bedroom and bath on each side.

Eric and Alison were embarrassed at having brought only their hand-clutch flight bags and her shoulder bag in the way of luggage. They were used to a more Spartan mode of travel.

"I don't even have a dinner dress to wear!" Alison moaned.

Before joining the prince before dinner, she suggested they try to contact Tom Peel by phone.

"Good idea," Eric nodded.

He dialed the ex-reporter's number. The ringing went on for a long time. Finally a woman's voice answered.

"I'd like to speak to Mr. Tom Peel, please," Eric said.

"Who's calling?"

"Mr. Peel doesn't know me, but my sister and I and a . . . a friend of ours are very interested in that old mansion in New Jersey called *El Gezirah*. We've read his newspaper stories about the house, and we'd like to—"

"I'm sorry, he's not here!" The voice said, followed by a loud click. Eric was left open-mouthed, cut off in mid-sentence.

"What happened?" Alison asked, seeing the look on his face.

"Whoever answered hung up." He put the receiver back in the cradle slowly, annoyed at the rudeness of the response.

"Man or woman?" said Alison.

"Woman. His wife, I suppose. Or a maid, maybe, though a maid probably would've been more polite."

"Didn't she give you any explanation?"

Eric shook his head. "Just said he wasn't there, and bang—down went the receiver!"

"Nasty, in a hurry, didn't care—what?"

"Funny, but I'd say she sounded . . . *scared.*"

In the glittering hotel dining room, during most of the meal, Haroun was so busy admiring Alison that the three young people reached the dessert course before the prince even thought to resume their conversation about the past history of *El Gezirah.*

"Tell me, please," he said, "what you learned at the newspaper office."

"Well, besides those disappearances the lawyer mentioned, while the McKee family was living in the house," Eric began, "at least four other people vanished there after the mansion became a museum. Only one ever turned up again."

"Inside the mansion?"

"No. This was several months later. He was found wandering in the woods nearby. The poor guy was out of his mind, just babbling—couldn't even give a clear account of where he'd been or what happened to him."

"Fantastic!" Haroun commented. "What about the others?"

Alison took up the story. The next victim, she said, was a man named Grodno. "One of the museum staff remembered seeing him enter the mansion, and his car was found parked outside at closing time. He was known to be mixed up in organized crime, so at first the police thought he might have been murdered by someone from another gang. But apparently that never happened at all. The enemy gang was as mystified by his disappearance as everyone else."

After Grodno came the case of a medical doctor, a well-known surgeon. His disappearance caused the state medical society to post a $25,000 reward, which was never claimed. Then a young woman vanished in the mansion— an aspiring actress with the improbable name of Cleopatra St. James.

"There was a rumor later on," said Alison, "that she drowned in a boating accident. But this was never proved."

"The fourth case," Eric said, "involved a businessman named Thule. It turned out his company was on the verge of bankruptcy, and friends said Thule was in a state of despair. The police thought he might have committed suicide, but if so, his body was never found."

The prince ordered Turkish coffee to finish the dinner. As they sipped the thick, sweet liquid from tiny cups, Haroun frowned. "Do you think Al Ghazali may also have disappeared forever?"

"I think," Alison said firmly, "that it's up to us to make sure he *doesn't*."

"Aha!" Prince Haroun smiled admiringly. "And have you any idea how this can be done?"

"For one thing, we can talk to the reporter who wrote those feature stories about *El Gezirah*. He may have some clues to the secret of the mansion that we know nothing about."

"I've already tried to call him," Eric added, "but his wife hung up on me. He lives here in New York City—across the East River in Queens. We thought we might go there this evening and find out why."

"Oh, but that is impossible!" Haroun exclaimed, glancing at his watch.

"Why?"

"Because we are all due at the theater in less than five minutes! We have front row center seats at the smash hit Broadway musical—*Falseface!*"

The Broadway/Times Square area was ablaze with twinkling lights and flashing neon signs. The Great White Way, it seemed, was still going strong.

The twins had to admit it was exciting being driven up to the theater entrance in an eye-popping royal limousine —especially when Captain Yusef Said sprang out in his Arab headdress and uniform to open the car door. Onlookers gaped and exclaimed.

The stage show, too, was lively and colorful—full of rousing, foot-tapping musical numbers. Nevertheless, when the stage lights faded to darkness between scenes, Eric and Alison could not help wondering and worrying about Al Ghazali. Not to mention those gun-toting impostors who had tried to ambush Prince Haroun!

The cast was just taking bows to thunderous applause at the final curtain when the theater manager stepped out on the stage. He raised his hands for silence.

"Ladies and gentlemen, I'm sorry to end the evening on a downbeat note, but I have a rather sad duty to perform. The theater has just had a telephone call from a Mr. Murdo McKee for the friends of Mr. A.G."

Murdo McKee? Eric and Alison stiffened in shock. Prince Haroun's mouth had dropped open in amazement.

"The friends of Mr. A.G.," the manager repeated, shading his eyes from the glare of the footlights in order to gaze out over the audience. Evidently he expected "the friends of Mr. A.G." to stand up and identify themselves. "The caller said that those friends would know whom the initials A.G. referred to. He asked us to inform them that A.G.'s condition is *very serious*. But he also promised to be in touch with further news as soon as possible."

The manager waited a few moments, looking around the theater. Both the prince and the Thorne twins, however, agreed it was wiser not to identify themselves.

"You can always call back from the hotel for more details," Alison whispered to Haroun.

As it turned out, no more details were forthcoming. When Prince Haroun telephoned the theater from his royal suite, he was referred to the manager's assistant, who had actually taken the sinister call. Haroun spoke to him for a few minutes, then slammed down the phone in disgust.

"The idiot cannot even describe the voice or remember how the caller sounded!"

"Probably wouldn't help us much, anyhow," Eric said gloomily.

"The message did speak of further news," Alison pointed out, trying to cheer up her two companions. "Maybe they'll call again, here at the hotel."

But no call came. Not that night, at any rate.

Next morning, the three teenagers were on their way to breakfast in the hotel dining room when the sallow-skinned, black-mustached diplomatic aide, Mr. Abu Kassim, arrived to speak to Prince Haroun. He brought stern orders from the Emir—transmitted by teletype from the royal palace on the Persian Gulf—instructing Haroun to help out in certain diplomatic activities of Hajar's delegation to the United Nations.

These chores, the Emir told his son, would help train him for his future royal duties.

"So it appears," Haroun told the twins over the breakfast table, "that I shall not be able to go with you to question that newspaper reporter."

"Never mind," Eric promised. "We'll handle it, and fill you in when we get back."

Tom Peel's address turned out to be a large, pleasant-looking brick house. It was located in a community called Douglaston, overlooking Little Neck Bay at one end of Long Island Sound.

A few seconds after Eric rang the bell, there was a rustle of curtains and a pair of eyes peered out.

Moments later, the front door opened on a chain, just wide enough for the twins to see a woman inside.

"Mrs. Peel?" said Eric.

"Who are you?"

"Eric Thorne. I called yesterday to speak to Mr. Peel."

"Oh, yes . . . so you're the one." The woman stared at Eric and Alison curiously.

"As I told you on the phone, my sister and I are interested in talking to him about the old mansion in New Jersey called *El Gezirah.*"

At the very mention of the name, the woman twitched as if she had just received an electrical shock. Her expression froze, and she drew back from the door.

"I'm sorry, Mr. Peel is out of the country," she snapped. "Next time he calls, I'll tell him you were here." The door slammed in their faces.

Eric knocked frantically.

The door opened again, approximately two inches.

"Please tell him we're staying at the Stuyvesant Plaza Hotel," Eric said hastily.

The woman shook her head. "I can't promise anything. But you can call back, if you like."

The door slammed again.

Eric looked at Alison.

"So much for Tom Peel," she said with a rueful grin.

The twins rode back gloomily to Manhattan on the subway.

"Thursday already," Eric said as the train rattled along. "I wonder when the Bears' coach is expecting Al Ghazali back."

Alison was thoughtfully silent. "Maybe he doesn't even know Al Ghazali came here," she mused aloud after a moment.

Eric gave her a pitying look. As if the coach wouldn't realize his star running back hadn't shown up for practice! Al must have made *some* arrangement to take time off and come east.

By now, they should have been driving home to Illinois, perhaps even arriving there, had all gone according to plan. What would the Bears' coach do when Al Ghazali failed to report back or even get in touch?

From the subway station, the twins walked back to the Stuyvesant Plaza, once again drinking in the vivid sights and sounds of Manhattan.

At the desk in the hotel lobby, the clerk behind the marble counter reported, "You had a call this morning, Mr. Thorne," and handed Eric a yellow slip of paper along with their room key. The note said:

The lawyer for the McKee Estate, Mr. G.
Humphrey Ward, called from Newark—has
some information for you. Please ring him
when you get in—before 12:00 if possible.

201-555-4647

6 • *The Shutterbug*

The twins hurried across the lobby to the elevators. One was just discharging its passengers. The twins stepped aboard and Eric pressed their floor button.

Alison fixed her brother with anxious brown eyes. "Do you suppose Al Ghazali's been found?"

Eric shrugged grimly. "Must be *something* important," he said. "Mr. Ward doesn't seem like the type to waste time on trivia."

"I wonder how Mr. Ward knew where to reach us?" she went on after a moment's silence.

"Probably through Haroun's people. Whoever first contacted him about buying *El Gezirah*."

"Come to think of it, that's rather odd, isn't it?" Alison said with a frown as the elevator door opened and they turned down the corridor toward their suite.

"How do you mean?"

"Calling us instead of them."

"Yeah, I guess it is. On the other hand, we're the ones who were asking him about *El Gezirah*."

Alison's luminous brown eyes sparkled. "Maybe he's found out something about those other disappearances!"

Eric turned the key and let them into their suite. Alison got an outside line on their room phone and dialed the law firm's number.

"Ah yes, Miss Thorne," said G. Humphrey Ward's dry precise voice, after his secretary put Alison's call through. "I'm sorry to say there's still nothing to report about the gentleman who's missing at *El Gezirah*. However, the real estate agency has arranged to keep someone on duty at the mansion at all times, in case of any developments. Meanwhile, I have just learned something that I thought might be of interest to you and your brother. Mind you, I'm not sure this can be of any help in—er, our present problem. Still, it may shed a little light when added to the results of your newspaper research."

"Then it has to do with the McKee mansion?" Alison asked, flashing a suspenseful look at Eric.

"Yes, with one of the disappearances there. You may recall my mentioning Murdo McKee's granddaughter?"

"Fiona."

"Correct. I see you've a good memory for names, Miss Thorne."

"She was engaged to marry a man named Jared Custer, you told us," Alison went on. "But then she disappeared. So Mr. Custer went to the police and got a warrant to have the mansion searched."

"Quite," said the lawyer, obviously impressed. "I believe I also told you that as far as I knew, she was never heard from again."

"You mean she *has* been?" Alison's eagerness caused the question to pop out impatiently.

"So it would seem." Mr. Ward explained that he'd had an early morning telephone conversation with the present heir to the McKee estate. The heir was an oil engineer who was working for one of the British petroleum-drilling firms now operating offshore in the North Sea. "I told him about yesterday's unfortunate incident—which in turn brought up the subject of previous missing-persons cases at *El Gezirah*. Much to my surprise, he told me his great-aunt Fiona evidently *did* survive."

"How did he know?"

"Ah, exactly! The key question. Unfortunately, the present heir wasn't too clear about that himself. But he's quite sure that, some time after Stuart McKee died—Stuart being Murdo McKee's son, you recall, and Fiona's father—one of his relatives either saw or heard from Fiona. The gist of their brief contact was that Fiona declared she had no interest whatever in the family estate, and she wouldn't even reveal where she was living."

"Wasn't your law firm acting for the McKees at that time?" Alison asked.

"Of course. Danforth, Ward and Milgrim has always served as the family's legal counsel."

"Yet the family didn't tell you Fiona had been heard from?"

"I'm afraid not." Mr. Ward's voice became drier than ever. "By that time, you see, Fiona McKee had long since been officially declared dead. I assume they thought it would simplify the probating of the estate if they just kept quiet about the matter. In any case, it made no difference to the outcome, since she wasn't even mentioned in her father's will."

"So now you have no idea whether or not she's still alive, or if so, where she may be living?"

"That is correct, my dear. But rest assured that you and your brother and the, uh, prospective purchaser of the mansion will be kept informed of any developments."

"Thanks ever so much, Mr. Ward. We certainly appreciate your call."

Alison put down the phone and relayed to Eric what the lawyer had told her. Then she pulled out the Manhattan directory from the telephone stand, plopped down in an easy chair, and began leafing through the book.

"What're you looking for?" her twin asked.

"Just want to see if there's any Fiona McKee listed."

"What makes you think she's living in Manhattan?"

"I don't, but there's no harm in looking, is there? If she's not in the book, we can check all the other directories in the New York metropolitan area."

Alison broke off presently with an irritated mutter. It sounded as though she'd failed to find the name she was looking for. But then she began flipping pages again.

Before Eric could find out what new scent she was off on, the telephone rang. He scooped up the handset.

"Hello?"

"*Subahkum bil'kheir,* Eric! Haroun here. Any luck this morning?"

"Zilch."

"I beg your pardon. What is zilch?"

"Zero, nothing—no luck at all. We saw the reporter's wife, but not him. Her latest story is that he's out of the country."

"Hmm. You find this strange?" Haroun inquired.

"Who knows? It could be true. What's strange is the way *she* carried on. When we rang the bell, she peeked out through the window first, then barely opened the door. And could hardly wait to slam it shut again!"

"Never mind, my friend. We shall have a delicious lunch—you and Alison and I—and talk of more pleasant things, OK?"

"Sounds great."

"I will send Yusef to pick you up. If you would not mind waiting for him down at the hotel entrance, that would be splendid. These pompous flunkies at my country's United Nations delegation are not allowing me much time for lunch. Indeed, they are acting offended because I do not choose to lunch with them. So time, as they say, is of the essence. OK?" Without waiting for any response, Prince Haroun hung up.

Grinning, Eric hung up the phone

As he did so, Alison exclaimed, "Hey! I think I've found her!"

"Who?" said Eric, unimpressed. "Someone named Fiona McKee?"

"Not just someone! I'll bet it's *her*—Stuart McKee's daughter!"

"What makes you so sure?"

"See for yourself," Alison insisted triumphantly.

When Eric walked over to look at the directory listing, he saw that her finger was pointing to the name *Jared Custer*.

"I thought you were looking up Fiona McKee," he objected.

"Jared Custer was the name of her fiance, remember?"

"Oh—right. But even so . . ."

"They were all set to be married, weren't they, the day she disappeared?" Alison argued. "And they must have been very much in love, if Custer even got a search warrant to hunt for his missing bride. If she didn't stay lost too long, isn't it logical they'd get back together again after she turned up—and go through with their interrupted wedding?"

"Hmm." Eric rubbed his chin. "Well, yeah—I suppose so, when you put it like that. But how do you know this is the right Jared Custer?"

"Oh, come on! How many Jared Custers can there be in this part of the country? Or the whole U.S.A., for that matter!" Alison tossed the directory down on the table.

"Now you've lost your place," he teased.

"So what? I've already memorized the number." She proved it by going back to the phone and dialing without hesitation.

After three rings, a female voice answered and repeated the number Alison had dialed. "He's not in at this time. May I take a message?"

"When do you expect him back?"

A confused silence ensued, as if this were an unfair question to throw at someone who was, after all, just answering the phone out of politeness. "I'm sorry . . . he left no word. He's probably out to lunch."

"Is this an answering service?"

"Yes, Ma'am. May I take a message?'

Alison sighed—"No thanks, I'll call back later"—and hung up in frustration.

"No luck?" Eric came out of his private bedroom and bath, where he had been hastily washing up and brushing his thick black hair. Now he was putting on a tie. "Come on! Haroun invited us to lunch, and Yusef's coming to pick us up. We're supposed to meet him downstairs."

"Now you tell me!" cried Alison in sudden panic. She jotted down Jared Custer's number, then darted across the suite to straighten up.

Outside the hotel, Alison watched the doorman help guests into and out of taxis and observed the pulsing waves of noontime traffic. Eric watched a red-haired girl standing on the island that divided Park Avenue. She was snapping pictures with a 35-millimeter camera.

Soon the girl lowered her camera and glanced back and forth at the buildings adjoining the Stuyvesant Plaza. Then after some traffic went past, she darted across the street toward them.

She moved this way and that, stopping and peering through the viewfinder, apparently trying to take a picture of the entrance. She was also an eyeful, a knockout—a fact that did not escape Eric's attention. Ringleted masses of reddish-gold hair, designer jeans, high-heeled boots. A couple of years older than Eric, but who cared?

"Do you want us to move?" Eric called to her. "I mean, we're just waiting for someone. We're not in the way, are we?"

"Oh no, not at all!" She smiled, and Eric's heart went

into overdrive. "In fact I kind of like it with you two standing there."

Alison regarded her brother coldly. He was acting like a nitwit. Her own smile was friendly enough however, as she turned back to the redhead.

"I'm a journalist, a photojournalist," she said. "Right now I'm working freelance for *Manhattan* magazine."

"What's your name?" asked Eric.

"Persia Palmer."

"*Persia?* That's your name—Persia?"

"Uh-huh. I know it's an odd name, but—"

"It's a terrific name!"

"You like it?"

"Fits you perfectly!" he said. She backed up a few steps, looking through the camera again.

"Are you working on a picture story right now?" he asked, trying hard to keep the conversation alive and delay the gorgeous redhead's departure. "Looks like you're shooting pictures of the hotel."

"Right. The Stuy Plaza's a marvelous example of Art Deco style architecture, you know—in fact one of the best in New York."

"You're into architecture?"

"Way in—that's my specialty! I do photographic studies of New York's most beautiful buildings. You know—trying to make the natives aware of the architectural glories all around them, so they won't think the city's only claim to fame is a bunch of skyscrapers. I started out studying architecture at N.Y.U., you see. But then I lost heart and got bitten by the camera bug. Trouble was, what really turned me on architecturally were these fantastic old Victorian mansions they used to build back around the turn of the century or before—but who wants any fantastic old mansions built nowadays?"

"Fantastic old mansions?" Eric echoed, a wild hope stirring.

Persia Palmer nodded enthusiastically. "Some of them are marvelous—the most imaginative edifices ever built in this country! If you ever saw one, you'd know what I mean. What I'm really hoping to do is put together a big coffee-table picture book showing some of these splendid houses in color—and telling the story behind each one. I've already done most of the research for it."

Eric shot a startled look at Alison, then turned back to the red-haired girl.

"You, uh—wouldn't happen to know anything about a house called *El Gezirah*, by any chance?"

"The old McKee mansion over in New Jersey?" Persia beamed. "Of course! As a matter of fact I know the architect's grandson."

Eric felt a thrill of excitement. "Does he live anywhere near new York?" he asked the red-haired photographer.

"The architect's grandson? Sure, he lives right in New York. In Brooklyn. Why?"

"We're sort of interested in *El Gezirah* ourselves. In fact we saw it just yesterday."

"Really?" Persia's bewitching green eyes grew even bigger. "Isn't that *something!* Oh, I wish I'd been there with you. Did you get inside?"

"Well—um—yes, we did. Apparently the house had a really strange history." Eric was picking his words carefully.

"I know—people disappearing and all that."

"Would the architect's grandson know anything about that?" put in Alison.

"About the disappearances?"

"About how they happened. I mean, like secret trap doors or whatever?"

"I certainly hope so! That's one of the things I want to talk to him about," declared Persia. Then she added, "Which I intend to do any day now, by the way."

"We're really interested in that house," Eric said. "We'd

ask you to have lunch or something with us in the hotel lounge, except that we're waiting for Prin—*urk!*"

His toe had just been stepped on. Hard.

"We'd love to have you join us for lunch"—Alison took over from her brother—"but we're waiting to be picked up. Since we're invited guests ourselves, I'm afraid it wouldn't be polite to bring someone else along."

"Of course. I understand," Persia said, smiling at Eric again. "Maybe some other time."

"Suppose we call you," Eric said with a fresh burst of inspiration. "Maybe we can still get together before Alison and I leave town."

"Oh, that would be great!" Persia brightened at once, and fished in her bag for pen and paper. "Actually I don't have a phone. I can't afford one. But this is the number of a coffee shop right next to my flat. The owner and waitresses are pals of mine, so I use it as an answering service." She giggled. "Whenever anyone calls and asks for Persia Palmer, they say, 'Just a moment, please,' and run next door to get me."

To Eric's chagrin, at that moment a big shiny black Lincoln Continental limousine glided up to the curb fronting the hotel marquee. Yusef was at the wheel.

"I'm sorry, we really must go now!" Alison exclaimed. "Here's the car we've been waiting for!"

She tugged Eric's arm, drawing him along with her.

"We'll be in touch!" Eric promised, waving at Persia with as jaunty an air as he could muster.

The redhead watched them climb into the limousine. A bit forlornly, Eric thought. He smiled and waved again as they sped off.

7 • The Bearded Spook

"You found her fascinating, I take it, " Alison grinned dryly.

Eric gave his sister a lofty glare. "Why the big rush to take off?"

"If we hadn't, you'd have stood there drooling over her for the next half hour."

Eric started to argue, then stopped with a brotherly qualm. Alison didn't have a jealous bone in her body; she was as wholehearted a Christian as any person he'd ever known. Nor did she spend any undue amount of time admiring or finding fault with her own image in the mirror.

So why such a tart reaction to Persia Palmer just now?

True, one of Alison's ambitions was to be a photo-journalist herself some day. But that was no cause for jealousy. On meeting an actual female news photog, he would normally have expected her to ask all sorts of eager questions and try to learn as much as she could. Not so with the devastating redhead, however.

Yusef dropped them at a Chinese restaurant near the United Nations. Prince Haroun was waiting at a corner table for three, and soon they were lunching on delicious *moo goo gai pan*—chicken with mushrooms.

After an exchange of news, Eric said, "Haroun, does Al Ghazali have any close relatives?"

"None that I know of. He is unmarried, and his parents are no longer alive. Why do you ask?"

"Just wondering if there's anyone we should notify about his disappearance. His team's coach is bound to start asking questions if he doesn't show up. There's that big game coming up this weekend with the Detroit Lions. Do you suppose he made any special arrangement to miss practice?"

The prince nodded. "Yes, I happen to know something about that. Mr. Abu Kassim—he is the diplomatic aide who met us at the hotel, you may recall—is married to an American lady, and partly because of her, he has become a fan of American football. So he was the one who contacted Al Ghazali and requested him to act as my father's agent in purchasing El Gezirah. And also, of course, to accompany us on the drive back to Illinois."

Haroun pronounced *Illinois* as if it rhymed with "choice." He explained that the football star had a slightly sprained ankle. He had not been taking part in team workouts, to give the sprain a better chance to heal.

Normally Al would have been required to attend the practice sessions, even though he remained on the sidelines. But at the special request of the U.S. State Department, his team manager had agreed to excuse him from practice on Wednesday and Thursday, so he could carry out an important confidential mission.

"So probably no one will start worrying about his absence until tomorrow—Friday," Eric reasoned.

"That seems correct," Haroun agreed. "I take it he is very important to his team's success?"

"You'd better believe it! Right now, Al Ghazali *is* the Chicago Bears. Their whole offensive strategy is built around his ground-gaining. With Al, the Bears are expected to win by at least two touchdowns. Without him, the Lions could score an upset."

"Therefore it is essential to his team that he be found quickly, eh?"

"And pretty essential to Al Ghazali himself, I should think," Alison put in wryly.

"Also important to the secrecy of Prince Haroun's visit," Eric pointed out. "If Al doesn't show up for practice Friday, the sports reporters will probably notice. If he's still missing Saturday, the day before the game, there'll be a *real* flap. By Sunday it'll be headline news. One way or another, I'll bet the news media would soon find out why he was missing."

"In which case," Haroun reflected gloomily, "my father, the Emir, would order me instantly back to Hajar. So I must insist that you two solve this case as soon as possible, please."

The twins chuckled—somewhat defensively.

"Just like that, huh?" said Eric.

"You now have—what? Two leads to work on?" Haroun persisted.

"Three, if we count the reporter who wrote the feature story on *El Gezirah*," Alison replied. "Other than him, there's Jared Custer in the Manhattan phone book, who *might* have been the fiance of Fiona McKee, the missing bride. And also this ravishing girl photographer, Persia Palmer, who claims to know the architect's grandson."

Eric thought he detected a sniff in his sister's voice when she mentioned the red-haired photographer—especially in the way she said those words *ravishing* and *claims*. But he kept his thoughts to himself.

"Why don't I try Jared Custer's number again?" Alison suggested as she finished nibbling her fortune cookie and spooning up the last of her ice cream. "Maybe he'll be back from lunch by now."

Alison excused herself from the table and went to a phone booth in a corner of the restaurant lobby to make the call. This time a man's voice answered.

"Yeah?" His tone was curt, but not unpleasant. He didn't sound old enough to have been engaged or married to Fiona, who by now—if Alison's hasty mental arithmetic was correct—must be somewhere in her fifties.

"Uh, this is rather hard to explain over the phone," Alison began. She wished now that she'd thought out beforehand exactly what to say, but the man's curt tone had rattled her.

"Then don't try, Luv," he said. "I'm in a mad rush."

"Wait! You *are* Jared Custer?" Alison went on hastily.

"You were expecting King Tut?"

"Does the name Fiona McKee mean anything to you?"

The speaker relaxed and chuckled. "It sure ought to!"

"Then could I please see you and talk to you?" Alison pleaded. "It's urgent, but I promise to make it brief."

"OK," he relented. "Around 2:30 would be best." And the receiver clicked down at the other end.

Alison hung up too, and returned to the table to report the result of her call. She found Eric and Prince Haroun poring over the rolled-up slips of paper that had been baked inside the Chinese fortune cookies.

Her own, which she'd glanced at before going off to telephone, said, *True beauty is more than skin deep.*

Haroun's said, *Look before you leap.*

Eric's said, *Beware of designing females.*

As Alison read this last one, Eric cocked a suspicious eye at his sister. "No wisecracks, please!"

"Did I say anything?" she replied innocently, but the corners of her mouth were twitching.

Prince Haroun, much to his frustration, had to resume his official chores with Hajar's U.N. delegation. But he promised to check back with the Thorne twins at the hotel as soon as he was free.

Alison announced her intention to go and talk to Jared Custer. His address in the West Thirties was within a pleasant walking distance of the restaurant.

For his own part, Eric decided there was no time like the present to learn whatever he could from the present-day descendant of the architect who had designed *El Gezirah*. So he stepped into the lobby phone booth Alison had just used and dialed Persia Palmer's number.

His pulse did a fast flutter when it turned out she was right there in the coffee shop.

"Eric!" she trilled. "How nice of you to call! And so soon!"

"Busy this afternoon?"

"Nothing I can't put off. What did you have in mind?"

"That architect's grandson you mentioned. Would he object to us dropping in on such short notice? Or even *no* notice?"

"Oh, no! I'm sure he'd be delighted. And why shouldn't he be, after all? Two such charming people as us!"

There was something about the way she said "us" that Eric liked very much. Already it was shaping up as a fun afternoon. "Where can I meet you?" he asked.

Persia gave him the location of the coffee shop. He promised to meet her there in twenty minutes.

Jared Custer's address turned out to be a lovely old Murray Hill townhouse of mellow red brick that showed to its best on this sunny autumn afternoon. It had been divided into several flats and offices, Custer's being on the third floor.

Alison rang his bell and waited, then rang again. She was about to ring for a third time when the inner door suddenly buzzed. She pushed it open and found an elevator in the inside lobby.

The town house was so narrow, there was only one

occupant per floor. Thus, when the elevator door opened to the third floor, Alison found herself already in Jared Custer's domain.

Her first glance left her confused. She had expected a residential apartment, or maybe an office. What she saw was neither. The room looked almost as bare as a gymnasium—that is, bare except for a cluster of spotlights, whose cables were snaked about the floor.

In the midst of the circle of lights, a man with a camera was snapping pictures of a rather stout but attractive woman in a pink pantsuit. As she turned and postured, the man with the camera kept barking out instructions and encouragement.

"A little left! Eyes up! C'mon, smile, Sugar! . . . That's it! Great! Perfect! Marvelous! . . . Now, try one hand on hip and turn a little more, so you're almost looking at me over your shoulder! . . . Whoops! Not quite so much! . . . That's it! Got it! . . . Right on! Terrific!"

Alison relaxed and grinned at her own slowness in catching on. Obviously this was a photographic studio. The man with the camera was shooting pictures of a fashion model—of the kind that was used to be called Stylish Stouts, but were now referred to as "B.B.W.," meaning Big Beautiful Women. Alison remembered once seeing a TV fashion show highlighting their new image.

The photographer abruptly finished shooting. "OK, that does it! Thanks a million, Lolly!"

He seized the model's hand and kissed it. At the same time he held out his camera. His assistant, who had been aiming the lights, took it and began unloading the film cartridge.

Meanwhile, the photographer turned and came striding toward Alison. "Now then! Let's have a look at you!"

He was a young man—in his late twenties, Alison judged—dressed in faded jeans and maroon velour pullover. Tall and wiry with a mop of blond hair.

He narrowed his eyes and began circling around Alison, viewing her from all angles. Then he took hold of her chin, gently but firmly, and tilted her head this way and that while he crouched and eyed her some more.

Alison was too astonished to resist.

"You sure aren't what I asked for," he muttered, "but you'll do . . . Oh, man, will you ever!"

"Are you Jared Custer?" she managed to ask.

"None other, Honey. The da Vinci of the fashion photogs! Did you bring your portfolio? Not that it matters! Hey, where'd you get those high cheekbones?"

"From my mother."

"What nationality?"

"American."

"No, I mean her ancestors, before they came over."

"They didn't have to come over," Alison grinned. "They were here. She was part Cherokee Indian."

"Honey, don't get me wrong, but I think you've got possibilities. With that skin and that bone structure, you were *made* for high fashion! Go on—get over there and try on that outfit! Let's see how it fits!" He pointed toward a dressing room cubicle in one corner of the studio.

Alison was about to protest and explain why she'd come. But then a spirit of mischief and adventure seized her. It might be fun to try her hand at fashion modeling! She would hardly have been human if she hadn't been flattered by Jared Custer's mistake.

Besides, when he found out who she really was, her willingness to pose might make him, in turn, more willing to answer questions about Fiona McKee's weird disappearance in *El Gezirah*.

With a twinkle in her dark topaz eyes, Alison headed for the dressing cubicle.

Persia's coffee-shop headquarters was on West 44th, on the fringes of the Broadway theater district. Her dazzling smile as he walked into the little restaurant made Eric's legs go slightly rubbery. She had to be just about the most beautiful creature he'd ever seen!

"Want some coffee?" she asked.

"Sure, I'll have a cup." He slid into the booth, across the little table from her.

Persia signaled the waitress.

"By the way, how do we get to this place in Brooklyn?" Eric asked after his coffee had been brought.

"You're not driving, are you?"

"Nope. But we can take a taxi."

"Don't be silly. Subway's faster and a lot cheaper. Though not as cheap as it used to be," she added with a rueful little grin.

"What's this man's name? The architect's grandson, I mean." It was the next thing that popped into Eric's mind. He was mostly trying to keep the conversation going.

"Northam, Harry Northam."

"Does he know we're coming?"

"Actually, no." Persia dimpled and blushed at the same time. Eric found this combination irresistible. "Look at it this way," she went on with a giggle. "If we call, he might say no. But if we just walk in on him, how can he turn us away?"

"Suppose he's out?"

"True, that's a risk we'll have to take. Of course if you'd rather not gamble that much time . . . "

"Hey, no! Nothing I'd like better!" Eric said hastily, meaning every word of it.

Persia lowered her emerald eyes and traced a squiggle on the table with her finger. When she looked up again, she seemed prepared to smile or hang her head in shame, depending on Eric's reaction. "Since you're being such a sport, I'd better level with you," she said.

"How do you mean?"

"The truth is, I don't know this Harry Northam. I've never seen him in my life."

Eric stared at her, not quite certain what to say.

"The man who designed the McKee mansion was an architect named Frederick Northam," Persia explained. "He's long gone, of course, but I checked him out through the Architectural Society and an old copy of *Who's Who* and, oh—all sorts of other references. Well, to make a long story short, I finally traced his present-day descendants. This Harry Northam, who lives in Brooklyn Heights, is his grandson—and honestly I *have* been meaning to look him up, like I said! I'm hoping he can tell me all about *El Gezirah* or whether his grandfather left any notes on the subject, but . . . anyhow, I just hadn't gotten around to it. Now that you're here, and you're interested in *El Gezirah* too—what could be a better time?"

Persia spread out her hands with a look of earnest innocence. Eric burst out laughing. So did Persia.

"Then you're not mad at me?" she said.

"What's there to be mad about? Let's get going!"

Persia steered them to the Port Authority Bus Terminal, which was only a few blocks away. The sidewalks were bustling with crowds of people, many of whom seemed to be thronging into or out of the terminal.

A stairway led down to the vast subway complex below street level. Here and there were magazine stands and grubby little shops. They bought subway tokens at a booth, then went through a downsloping tunnel whose walls were plastered with advertising posters.

As they waited on the subway platform for a train, Persia nudged Eric. "Are you being guarded or followed or something?"

He wasn't sure whether her whispered question was serious or joking.

"Not that I know of. Why?"

74

"Don't look now, but there's a character standing by that pillar who keeps watching us when he thinks we're not looking." Persia added with an impish grin. "At least I *think* he's watching us. With those dark glasses he's wearing, it's hard to be sure. His whole getup looks like a comic opera disguise!"

Eric waited a while, then casually looked around as if surveying the whole train platform.

Sure enough, a man with dark glasses was standing by the nearest pillar. He had bushy eyebrows, a handlebar mustache and muttonchop whiskers that joined the tips of his mustache. Something clicked in Eric's memory.

Where had he seen that man before?

The whole station rumbled and echoed with the roar of an incoming Number 2, Seventh Avenue express. The train stopped and its doors slid open. People swarmed out. Others swarmed in.

As the doors slammed shut again and the train moved on, Eric saw that the man with the dark glasses had boarded the same car. A chill flickered down Eric's spine, and the short hairs bristled at the nape of his neck.

He had just remembered where he'd seen such a face before.

It was in the foyer of *El Gezirah,* looking down from that oil portrait of Murdo McKee!

8 • Subway Tag

Cool it, boy! Eric told himself. *Let's not start imagining things!*

It had to be just an accidental resemblance. Old Murdo McKee was long since dead and laid to rest. Even if any family resemblance persisted, his current heir was three or four thousand miles away, working on an oil rig in the North Sea.

All the same, except for the dark glasses, this subway rider certainly *did* look like Murdo McKee. Spookily like him!

And Persia said he'd been watching Eric on the platform.

One of those two facts might be shrugged off. Together, they had to be more than coincidence!

There was one way to test his suspicions. By now the train had stopped at 23rd Street and was under way again. As it slowed for its next stop, Eric seized Persia's hand. "Let's get off!"

"But we're not there y—"

"Come on!" He tugged her to her feet. "I'll explain later!"

They squirmed their way out of the crowded car and

headed for the exit turnstiles. Eric glanced over his shoulder and felt a rush of adrenaline that gunned his pulse. The man in dark glasses was hastily leaping out of the subway car before its door closed.

It could still be coincidence, Eric tried to tell himself.

Two flights of stairs led up to street level from the tiled underground station. Eric chose one at random. He rushed Persia up the steps, squirming past the people going up or coming down. With luck, they might be out of sight before their shadow could follow them topside!

Reaching the street, Eric looked around the intersection. "Where does that other flight of stairs come up?"

Looking puzzled, Persia pointed across the street. "Over there."

"Come on!" Eric hustled her across 14th Street as the traffic light was turning yellow, then down the stairs and back into the subway station.

"I don't get it," Persia murmured breathlessly. "What are we playing—ring-around-the-rosy?"

"I think that guy with the dark glasses is tailing us!"

They had bought return tokens at the Port Authority terminal, so they had two left. They used these to get back through the turnstile.

"Oh—" Persia whispered moments later, as they waited on the platform. "You were right! Here he comes again!"

Eric darted a quick glance. The bearded spook was just dropping a token in the slot, about to follow them onto the platform—the same platform they had left only minutes earlier.

"Who is he? What's this all about?" Persia asked under her breath.

Eric could only shrug. "Dunno. Since he's wearing that disguise, it must have something to do with *El Gezirah.*"

Persia's green eyes showed her puzzlement. She started to say something, then seemed to change her mind and instead said simply, "What are *we* going to do?"

"Try to shake him somehow. Let me think."

Ten minutes went by before another train came rumbling through the tunnel. During that time, the man with dark glasses had shown no interest in the young couple. But Eric had no doubt he was fully aware of their presence and of any move they might make.

By now other people had collected on the platform. The man who looked like Murdo McKee was standing a few yards away from Eric and Persia as the incoming train thundered to a halt. A number of passengers got off. Out of the corner of his eye, Eric saw their shadow getting into the same car he and Persia were boarding, but through the other door.

Persia headed for a vacant seat, but Eric gripped her arm and held her back. "Stay close to the door!" he muttered.

Everyone was aboard now—the doors would soon close.

"Come on!" Eric hissed. At the last moment, he darted off the train again, tugging Persia with him. The bearded spook followed suit, exiting through the other door.

But as the doors began to slide shut, Eric suddenly reversed himself. Blocking the door with one elbow and shoving Persia in front of him, he squeezed back aboard— in the barest nick of time before the doors slammed shut!

The train jerked into motion. Eric had the satisfaction of seeing Murdo McKee's bearded double glare at them furiously as the subway cars rumbled off into the tunnel.

"We did it!" Persia chuckled, squeezing Eric's hand. "We shook him! Or you did, rather. Pretty neat!"

The conductor came and lectured them on the dangers of jumping in and out of closing subway doors, including a few unpleasant examples of people who had tried it unsuccessfully. By now other passengers were regarding the young couple with curious stares, but not for long. New Yorkers were used to weird goings-on, and considered it safer to mind their own business. By the time the express reached its next stop in lower Manhattan, what had happened at the 14th Street station was ancient history.

Two stops later, Eric and Persia got off at Clark Street in Brooklyn. By asking directions, they soon found the address they were looking for—a well kept brownstone. A gray-haired, kindly-looking man in his sixties answered their ring.

"We're looking for Mr. Harry Northam," Eric said.

"You've found him, Son."

"I, uh, believe your grandfather was the architect, Frederick Northam?"

"Nope, wrong party. My grandfather on that side of the family was a lock tender on the Erie Canal."

The reply was so unexpected that Eric's jaw dropped open. He looked at Persia, whose face showed equally blank surprise.

"But there must be some mistake!" she exclaimed. "I traced Frederick Northam's descendants very carefully. He lived in Brooklyn after he retired, and his grandson's name was Harry. And there's only one Harry Northam in the Brooklyn directory."

"That may be so, Miss," said the elderly man. "But that doesn't make me a descendant of Frederick Northam."

Persia's lovely green eyes looked ready to fill with tears, and her lower lip was trembling. "But someone at the Architectural Society said you *were* the right Northam," she quavered.

"Sorry, little lady. Anyone can make a mistake."

It was terribly hot and uncomfortable under the lights. Alison had been striking and holding poses for what seemed like hours, always conscious of the camera lens eyeing her critically—first from one angle, then another.

But she was having the time of her life!

When she'd first gone into the dressing cubicle, the BBW model was still changing into street clothes. Alison was afraid she might start asking embarrassing questions and expose the fact that this teenager was a fake and an amateur, with no modeling experience.

Instead, the stout woman had been friendly and encouraging, gushing out admiring comments. "Oh, Honey —aren't you *perfect* for showing off these young fashions! Just a *natural,* if I ever saw one. With your face and figure, I'll bet Jared has you on magazine covers in six months! . . . Tell me, Sweetie, is this your first job?"

Alison blushed nervously. "As a matter of fact, yes."

"Don't worry about a thing, dear. I can tell you right now, you're going to be sensational!"

She was hoping that the costume would be something dressy or unusual, maybe a formal or party dress that would make her feel like a—well, like a jet set cover girl. But it turned out to be a simple button-front cotton dress in a rust-colored plaid.

Alison's spirits sank . . . until she stepped out of the dressing cubicle and saw Jared Custer's reaction.

"Hey, all right! That number was made to order for you!"

The dress certainly fitted like a glove. And its rusty plaid was ideal for her black tresses and dark complexion.

The makeup man had been out of the studio, getting coffee and sandwiches. When he came back and saw Alison's face, which he would now prepare for the camera, he became semi-ecstatic.

"My dear Jared, she is a work of art already! Who could possibly improve that nose, that bone structure! What a divine little creature we have here!"

Opening his makeup kit, he began deftly applying cosmetics. "With her marvelous skin tone, we need almost no foundation makeup. Just a hint of rouge to highlight the cheekbones . . . some lip gloss, of course, for smoothness and luster, and perhaps the merest touch of eyeliner and shadow, just to dramatize these huge, luminous brown orbs!"

Jared insisted on taking her hair out of its ponytail and tossing it wildly about her head.

When Alison saw the results in a mirror, she could hardly believe her eyes. By the time she took her place in front of the camera, Alison had lost all her fears. She twirled and postured and fluffed out her hair with both hands as if she'd been posing for fashion photographers all her life.

Jared kept shouting out orders—wheedling, praising, encouraging. "Left leg out—let your foot rest on the heel! . . . That's it! Great! . . . Now, turn to your right! Laugh, giggle! Toss your head! . . . Perfect! Terrific!"

He wound up shooting three rolls of film. When he was halfway through the third roll, another model arrived—obviously the girl for whom he'd mistaken Alison.

At first Jared was just as confused and bewildered as she was over the situation. But after a few moments sorting things out, he soothed the other model and sent her off with promises of full pay and another assignment very soon.

Then he turned back to Alison with a wry grin. "So you're the girl who phoned me and asked about Fiona McKee!"

She nodded. "You told me to come at 2:30."

"I know, I know!" Jared Custer slapped his forehead and looked chagrined. "I figured there'd be time to talk between the two shooting sessions. Leave it to me to get absentminded!"

"I—I'm sorry I didn't speak up and explain," Alison faltered guiltily.

"Don't be! Who's complaining, Honey? It isn't every day I make a discovery like you. This could be the start of something beautiful. Believe me, you've got a brilliant modeling career ahead, if you want one! But never mind all that now. First, tell me who you *really* are, and where you heard the name Fiona McKee."

When she explained how she and her brother were hoping to solve the mystery of the old McKee mansion, Jared chuckled.

"Dunno if I can help you much on that. Fiona McKee was my mother's maiden name. All I ever heard was that she and my dad eloped—and her old man practically had apoplexy! But give me a chance to think . . ."

It was past four o'clock when Eric returned to the Stuyvesant Plaza. He had parted reluctantly from Persia, wishing their date could stretch on through dinner and into the evening. But he felt it his duty to check in with Alison and Prince Haroun.

Much to his annoyance, neither had returned to the hotel. Eric was reduced to watching late-afternoon television fare while he waited for them to show up. Haroun arrived soon after five p.m., looking peevish and out of sorts. Obviously diplomatic handshaking and sitting through long speeches at the U.N. General Assembly had not improved his temper. But he listened with keen interest to Eric's report of his visit to Harry Northam and the weird incident involving Murdo McKee's look-alike.

It was almost 5:30 when the room phone rang. Alison was calling from Jared Custer's studio.

"What's keeping you?" Eric inquired.

"Believe it or not, I've been fashion modeling all afternoon."

"Fashion modeling?"

"Don't sound so surprised. I'm really good at it, or so Jared Custer tells me. He's a fashion photographer."

"Did you get to meet his wife?"

"No, and she's not his wife. This is Jared Junior. Fiona McKee is his mother."

"OK, great," Eric retorted impatiently. "But what's that got to do with *El Gezirah?*"

"Well," said Alison, "It's a long story. I'm hoping she can explain the secret of all those disappearances. But first he has to get in touch with her."

"So? What's the problem?"

"It's not a simple as it sounds. His parents are in England. Jared's been trying to get a call through. Meantime, we thought we'd pop out for a quick bite. Could you and Haroun excuse me from dinner? I'll come back to the hotel as soon as I have something to report."

"Uh, well—OK." Eric put down the phone and plowed his fingers through his thick black hair in sheer bewilderment.

Haroun looked nettled when he heard how Alison had blossomed into a fashion model and was about to dine with her photographer. "Do you think it is proper," he demanded, "allowing her to dine with some strange man she has never met before?"

Eric could only shrug. "They certainly must be acquainted by now, if she's been posing for him all afternoon. Besides, Alison's a sensible girl. I trust her judgment."

The two youths went out to a nearby Italian restaurant. A delicious meal of lasagna put them both in a much better frame of mind.

The telephone was ringing when they got back to their hotel suite an hour later.

Eric snatched up the handset, expecting to hear Alison's voice. To his delight, Persia Palmer was on the line. But she sounded strangely subdued, compared to the vivacious redhead whom he'd met earlier that day.

"The friend you and your sister lunched with—would he be an Arab, by any chance?" Persia inquired.

Eric was taken aback. "Well, yes, as a matter of fact. Why?"

"I have a letter for him."

"A *letter?*" Eric was now utterly baffled. "I—I don't understand. How come?"

"When I got home," Persia explained, "I didn't go right up to my room. I stopped off a the coffee shop first to see if there were any messages. Then one of my girlfriends came in and we wound up having supper. Anyhow, when I finally got back to my flat, I found this envelope shoved under my door. It's addressed to 'Eric Thorne's Arab Friend.'"

Eric felt a twinge of uneasiness and alarm. It seemed likely that the envelope must have been left by that bearded spook who'd tailed them on the subway. Which meant their unknown shadow must not only know about the Thorne twins' interest in *El Gezirah,* but also Prince Haroun's connection with the old mansion!

"Eric, I don't like this," Persia was saying. "Especially after that nut followed us! What's this all about?"

"It's, uh . . . a little hard to explain over the phone," Eric stalled. "Wait'll I see you in person, then I'll tell you as much as I can. I'll be right over to pick up the letter."

"All right. You needn't ring, by the way. The inside front door locking my apartment building got broken this afternoon, so just walk in. I'm in 309. Come on up and knock—I'll be expecting you."

"OK. See you in a little while, Persia!"

Haroun had overheard enough to pique his curiosity. Eric hung up and relayed the news.

"*Bismillah!*" the prince exclaimed. "This could be another message from whoever called the theater last night! He promised we would hear from him again!"

Eric nodded tensely. "Could be. But it's a funny way to get in touch!"

"True. But then having an announcement read aloud on stage is not the most usual way to communicate, either."

Eric had to grin. "You've got a point there, pal!"

He left a note for Alison, in case she returned to the hotel while they were gone. Then Haroun called his limousine, and Yusef drove the two youths to Persia Palmer's apartment building on West 44th. Even though Eric hadn't seen her home to her door, she had pointed the place out to him when they left the coffee shop earlier that afternoon.

As Persia had said, the front door lock was broken, so they entered without bothering to ring. There was no elevator in the inside lobby, and the walls were scrawled with graffiti. Obviously the building was not exactly in the luxury class.

Eric and Haroun climbed three flights of stairs and found 309. The door of the flat stood ajar. Eric gave a couple of gentle knocks. Then, hearing no response, he called out, "Persia?"

Again no answer.

Eric felt the first pang of alarm. He pushed the door wide open and walked in, shouting her name.

A quick glance around sufficed to show him the flat was empty. But an envelope lay on the floor at their feet.

Prince Haroun picked it up and opened it. The hand-lettered message inside said:

WAIT FOR CALL IN YOUR HOTEL ROOM.
FOR A.G.'S SAKE, TELL NO ONE!

9 • Skyscraper Caper

Without a word, Haroun handed the message to Eric, who scanned it quickly.

"Looks like your guess was right. This must be from the same person who called the theater."

Haroun nodded grimly. "I agree. But what of your red-haired lady friend?"

"Not here. Don't ask me why. I suppose she could've just stepped out for a moment. Maybe down the hall to speak to a friend, or something like that."

"But you don't think so."

Eric shrugged, his expression clearly reflecting his concern. "I don't know what to think, Haroun. I don't see any signs of a struggle, as if she'd been kidnapped. On the other hand, she knew we were coming, and she did promise to be here, so it's strange that she isn't. Maybe that's why she left her door open—meaning she'd be right back."

They sat down to wait, but not very calmly. From time to time, one or the other would get up to pace the floor. at one point, Eric even stuck his head out of the door and shouted, *"Persia!"* in hopes that she might be somewhere within hearing distance. But she failed to respond.

After ten or fifteen minutes, Prince Haroun's impatience began to show. And Eric himself was troubled about Persia, with a feeling he couldn't quite pin down. The more he thought about it, the more coincidental it seemed that this pretty redhead should accost him and Alison in front of the hotel—and then *just by chance* turn out to be interested in old mansions like *El Gezirah!*

Every instinct told Eric that beautiful green-eyed Persia Palmer was no crook. All the same, how could he be sure? And why wasn't she here to meet him and Haroun?

"Come on, let's go." Eric suddenly leaped to his feet. "I'll leave a note for Persia. Maybe it's just as well, anyhow, if we don't talk to her. This way we don't have to explain who you are or what the message is all about."

"You are right," Haroun agreed. "That may be wisest."

Nevertheless, just to make sure, Eric checked the coffee shop before they left. One of the waitresses told him Persia had not been back since dinner.

"OK, thanks. If you do see her, tell her Eric stopped by."

The sun was down, and in the deep purple dusk Manhattan was lighting up for the evening as Yusef whisked them back to the Stuyvesant Plaza in the royal limousine.

Haroun inquired at the desk and learned there had been no calls in his absence. Alison, however, had returned. The two boys stopped long enough to collect her from the twins' suite before moving on to Prince Haroun's sumptuous quarters.

"Now, what's all this about you fashion modeling for Jared Custer—or Jared Jr.?" said Eric when they were all comfortably seated.

"He mistook me for a model he was expecting," Alison replied, "so I went along just for fun. And it was!"

Seeing Haroun glowering jealously, she added, "I also thought it might help me persuade him to help *us* find out why all those people have disappeared at *El Gezirah.*"

"Well, did it?" Eric pursued.

"Oh, yes, Jared's going to help—in fact, he's already helped! But it's going to take time to get the full answer."

"How come?"

Alison explained that Mr. and Mrs. Jared Custer, Sr., were on vacation in England. They were staying at a hotel in London. But when their son had called them there, he learned they had started out yesterday on a motor tour of the country. The hotel, which had arranged the tour, tried to track them down.

"Jared finally got hold of them at a little country inn in the Cotswold Hills. But it was almost midnight over there, and besides, the connection was terrible. When Jared talked to his mother—Fiona, that is—he could hardly understand what she was saying."

"Well, what *did* she say?" Eric demanded impatiently.

"First of all, she knew right off what he was talking about when he told her someone else had just disappeared at *El Gezirah*. And if Jared understood her correctly, she said that she herself had disappeared *on purpose*—to keep her father from stopping her marriage."

"I thought her disappearance did stop the marriage."

"Only temporarily. After she returned from wherever she'd disappeared to, she rejoined her fiance and they went through with their wedding. But she didn't get back in touch with her family for years. She didn't even let them know she was alive, for fear her father might try to hurt Jared or both of them."

"Sounds like a rather nasty fellow," said Haroun.

"Oh, he was!" said Alison. "Both he and her grandfather, old Murdo McKee! Like father, like son, I guess. Meantime, of course, everyone assumed Fiona was dead. When her father found out she wasn't, he disowned her and refused to speak to her again."

"But *how* did she disappear?" put in Eric, sticking to the point.

"I don't know," Alison admitted. "That's when the connection got really bad. Her voice was fading in and out, so Jared could barely make out what she was saying. Finally she told him it would take too long to explain over the phone, anyway, and the simplest thing would be to read the whole story for himself."

Both of Alison's listeners looked puzzled.

"What does *that* mean?" Haroun inquired.

"Apparently old Murdo McKee never told anyone—not even his son Stuart—about the house's disappearing trick, but he did keep a private journal or diary that told all about it. And Fiona stumbled on it not long before she became engaged to Jared. In this journal, her grandfather told how he himself used to vanish when he wanted to dodge creditors or business enemies, or stall on some business deal he didn't want to go through with. And that's what gave Fiona the idea of disappearing when her father threatened to stop her marriage."

"And this old journal still exists?" Eric asked eagerly.

"Yes. She took it with her when she disappeared—to make sure none of her family might read it and discover the trick. Jared—I mean Jared Jr., the photographer—remembers seeing it around the house. His mother said to read pages 43 through 47 and he'd know everything."

"Dynamite!" Eric exclaimed, flashing a jubilant smile at Haroun. "And how soon do we find out the great secret?"

"Jared's parents live up in Westchester County," Alison replied. "That's just north of New York City. Jared's going to drive me up to their house tomorrow afternoon and let me read those pages."

"Tomorrow afternoon? That's cutting it pretty close," said Eric with a worried frown. "By that time, the Bears' coach could be raising the roof because Al Ghazali hasn't reported back for practice!"

Before anyone could comment, the telephone rang, electrifying Haroun and the twins.

The prince, who was sitting nearest the telephone, picked up the handset. "Yes!"

"Am I speaking to the young man from Hajar?" It was a male voice speaking in a hoarse whisper, so that Haroun could not guess the caller's age or type.

"Yes. Who is this?"

"Never mind who I am! Just listen. I must talk fast. Are you interested in finding Mr. Al Ghazali?"

"Of course!"

"Then pay careful attention. I can give you these instructions only once—and let me add, Mr. Ghazali's safety may depend how well you follow them. At exactly midnight tonight, be on the penthouse terrace on top of the Crescent Oil Building in Manhattan. Look all around. You'll see a blinking light. Be ready for it."

"A blinking light?"

"Don't interrupt me or I'll hang up. Understand? There'd better be no one else on the roof terrace but you. The roof lighting will make it easy to see, and I don't want to spot any sniper—ready to take potshots when the light starts blinking. For Al Ghazali's sake, this is your one and only chance to help him."

"Wait!" exclaimed Prince Haroun. "Are you talking about a light in a window of one of the buildings—"

"I can tell you nothing more. Walk around if you like. You'll see it."

The receiver clicked down at the other end of the line.

Prince Haroun hung up slowly. His desert-tanned face was a study in mingled hope and frustration as he reported the conversation to the Thorne twins. "I do not understand. I assume he means there will be a message in code, but I do not know International Morse Code! I suppose I can write down what I see . . ." he shrugged.

"What are you going to do?" Eric asked uneasily.

"Carry out the caller's instructions, of course. Al Ghazali would never have disappeared had he not been doing my father and me a favor. How can I refuse to take any step which may help us find him safely?"

"Will your father permit it?" Alison ventured to ask.

Haroun's reply was almost scornful. "Do you think any true member of the Royal House of Hajar would turn his back on a faithful friend?"

"The Crescent Oil Building," Alison went on. "Where is that?"

"Not far from the United Nations. It is a skyscraper which belongs to the Oil Corporation of Hajar. That is the official name of our country's petroleum firm, although it is more commonly known as Crescent Oil. The corporation occupies the top five floors."

Prince Haroun called his diplomatic aide, Abu Kassim, who was staying in another room there at the Stuyvesant Plaza. Haroun ordered Kassim to summon Hajar's U.N. Ambassador, Mehmet Farouk, to the hotel at once for an urgent conference.

While the three young people waited, Eric related his own adventures that afternoon. He was still worried about Persia Palmer, so he took time to call the coffee shop. Several minutes after answering, a waitress came back to the phone and told him Persia was not in her flat.

Eric hung up, feeling even more uneasy than before his call. He got up and wandered around the royal suite.

"I'll admit it's odd that she wasn't there when you went to pick up the letter," Alison commented.

Eric scratched his head. "You're suspicious of her . . . aren't you?"

Alison hesitated. On the surface, Persia had seemed so pleasant and high-spirited. All the same . . .

"Yes," she admitted. "It just seemed a bit much, the way she recognized us and came up and talked to us—and then just by chance it turned out she's also interested in the McKee mansion."

Eric snapped his fingers. "OK, you've just brought up

something that's been bothering me too. Did you get the impression she'd ever visited *El Gezirah?*"

"Well, of course. Don't you remember her reaction when you told her about us going there—the way she gushed, 'Isn't that something?' As if she were comparing notes. So we could understand why the house turned her on so much."

Eric nodded. "Right. And if she'd been there, she must surely have seen that portrait of Murdo McKee."

"I'd certainly think so," Alison agreed.

"Yet now that I think of it, she never seemed to catch on to the resemblance between the bearded spook and the portrait—or why I figured he must have something to do with the *El Gezirah* mystery! She just didn't get the connection. But how could she miss it, when the guy looked just like Murdo McKee wearing dark glasses?"

"Perhaps she saw the portrait some time ago," Haroun spoke up, "so now she has forgotten how he looked. Or perhaps she has seen *El Gezirah* from the outside, but never inside when it was open as a museum."

"Hmm." Eric had to admit that what Haroun said seemed reasonable. "That could explain it, I suppose."

"Another question," Haroun mused aloud. "One might ask, why this whole elaborate—er, buildup? Is that not how you Americans say—buildup? I mean why send me that mysterious letter through the young lady, telling me to expect a call? Why not simply telephone me, without announcing the call beforehand?"

"Maybe to make sure you'd be here to answer," said Alison. "Or to impress on us beforehand that the call was important—so you'd be sure to take it seriously. Come to think of it, that spook Eric saw, who made himself up with fake whiskers to look like old Murdo McKee, was probably the same person who called just now. I'll bet the disguise was meant to convince us that he really knew the secret of *El Gezirah!*"

"Good thinking, Allie," Eric nodded approvingly. "I have a hunch you've hit the nail right on the head."

Further discussion was cut short by the arrival of the two Hajarite diplomats, accompanied by Haroun's bodyguard, Yusef Said. Ambassador Farouk was alarmed when he heard about the mysterious telephone call, and the plan requiring Prince Haroun to watch for a blinking light from atop the Crescent Oil skyscraper.

"Your father, the Emir, would never agree!" the plump, bearded Arab exclaimed, dabbing his brow nervously with a handkerchief.

"On the contrary," said the prince, "I am confident he *would* agree. I believe he might even consider it my *duty!*"

"Perhaps," put in the sallow, mustached aide, Abu Kassim, "we could have have the top floors of the building, as well as the penthouse and terrace, all thoroughly searched beforehand by our security guards. We could also post armed guards at all stairways and elevators. In this way, we could prevent any danger of a surprise attack by assassins while His Highness is alone on the roof, watching for the light."

"Excellent thought, Kassim!" said the prince.

"But that is not the only way an attack could occur," Ambassador Farouk protested to Haroun. "Your caller, you say, wishes you to be alone on the roof when the light appears. How do we know your caller is not planning to make you an assassin's target?"

"Because he could have killed me much more easily when I went to Miss Palmer's flat to get the letter. A gunman could have been hiding inside and shot both Eric and myself when he walked in the door. With a silencer on his gun, he would have been far away before the crime was discovered."

There was a moment of grim silence. Eric felt a chill in the pit of his stomach as he realized how easy such an ambush would have been.

"I believe the prince has made a shrewd point, Your Excellency," Kassim said to the ambassador. "If I may offer a suggestion—does not His Highness possess a bulletproof vest?"

"Kassim is right—I do!" said Haroun, his face brightening. "My father insists that I take one whenever I travel outside of Hajar. And not only a bulletproof vest—there is also a special protective helmet, which Yusef carries in the royal limousine."

Ambassador Farouk considered, then turned to Captain Yusef Said, who had been listening impassively to the discussion. "You are the prince's bodyguard, Captain. What have you to say about all this?"

The giant Arab shrugged. "The final decision must rest with His Majesty, the Emir, of course. As for myself—if the prince does indeed carry out this plan at midnight, I make only one request."

"And what is that, Yusef?" Haroun inquired.

"That I be allowed to station myself just inside the penthouse door—suitably armed with automatic weapons, and a high-powered target rifle with sniperscope."

"Granted!"

The night was overcast and windless. Prince Haroun paced restlessly about the rooftop terrace, wondering how much longer he would have to wait. Far below, glancing down over the parapet, he could see Madison Avenue—yellow-streaked with the headlight beams of passing cars as midnight approached.

The helmet was a nuisance. Still, it left his eyes and nose uncovered and did not hamper his vision.

Here and there, windows still glowed brightly in the jagged, upthrusting skyscrapers that loomed on all sides. But as yet he had glimpsed no blinking light.

Haroun paused to peer at the luminous dial of his expensive, wafer-thin wristwatch . . . 11:58.

The time was getting close! Surely it would not be much longer now before the signal came. Unless his unknown informant was engaged in some mysterious war of nerves —or the whole episode turned out to be a hoax.

The Emir had made little objection to the plan. As Haroun had expected, he seemed to accept it as a princely duty that his son should do whatever might be necessary to hasten the safe return of the Hajarite-American hero— football star and air ace, Al Ghazali.

He had disappeared in the service of the Emir, therefore it behooved the—

Haroun stopped abruptly and cocked his head skyward. He had just heard the distant clatter of a helicopter.

It was coming this way.

The craft gradually took shape out of the darkness. Then a light began flashing . . .

The blinking light!

Haroun tensed with excitement. *Bismillah!* All along he had been anticipating a signal that would flash from a window of one of the surrounding skyscrapers. Whoever planned this operation had taken him and his counselors completely by surprise!

The helicopter was swooping lower. But what sort of signal was meant? The light was simply flashing on and off in a jerky irregular rhythm. Surely this was not Morse code!

A sudden dazzling glare lit up the darkness. Without warning, the blinker had been replaced by a high-powered spotlight! And it was aimed directly at him!

Shielding his eyes from the blinding white radiance, Haroun felt a surge of panic—and awareness that he might be in mortal danger!

"Yusef! *Ehrug!*" he cried. *"Gahyee! Gahyee! Hawinnee!"*

Even as he shouted for help, there was a loud *splat!*

nearby—as if something had been thrown from the 'copter and had landed hard on the rooftop.

A gas grenade!

Acrid fumes billowed in all directions. Haroun found himself coughing and choking. He clapped one hand over his nose and screwed up his eyes tightly, but tears were already streaming out from underneath his lids. At the same time, Yusef came charging out of the penthouse in answer to his master's cries. He was clutching an assault rifle—ready to spray lead in any direction! But the glare and dense gas fumes blinded him.

The helicopter made an audible target. From the loudness of the rotor racket, it was evidently touching down on the rooftop. But Yusef feared to trigger a burst, lest Prince Haroun be in his line of fire.

An armed man wearing a gas mask jumped out of the chopper. Neither Haroun nor Yusef could see him. Yusef felt something sprayed in his face, and an instant later he began to retch violently.

A net was thrown over Haroun. He struggled in helpless fury, but it was no use. He was quickly trussed and loaded into the aircraft.

Haroun heard the rotor take on a deeper, stronger note. In seconds, the helicopter was soaring off into the night sky!

10 • Nasty News

An anxious group was waiting in the executive suite on the top floor of the Crescent Oil skyscraper. U.N. Ambassador Mehmet Farouk and his diplomatic aide, Abu Kassim, had set up a midnight command post there with the head of the building's security force, and the Thorne twins had been allowed to join them at Prince Haroun's express command.

It was now 12:09.

As the appointment time for the blinking-light signal came and passed, tension mounted swiftly. The company switchboard was being manned by a security guard. A direct line connected the president's office, where the group was waiting, with the penthouse on the roof, where Captain Yusef Said had been posted out of sight.

Farouk mopped his brow nervously. "This whole business was a mistake, a bad mistake!" he fretted. "I feel it in my bones! We should never have allowed the prince to expose himself in this way!"

"Relax, sir. You've got a good man up there in Captain Said," said the building security chief. "If anything fishy develops, he'll be right on top of the situation!"

"Then why has he not yet reported? We dare not wait any longer! I shall call him right now!" He reached for the phone on the company president's desk.

"Wait, Mr. Ambassador!" said Eric. "If anything's happening up there, Captain Said may have his hands full. Isn't there danger that the telephone ringing may distract him at just the wrong time?"

"Hmm, yes—perhaps you are right." Farouk let go of the phone. "Nevertheless, I think it most urgent that we check with him immediately!"

He raised his hand and snapped his finger at a uniformed guard who was standing in the doorway.

"Take the elevator to the penthouse and find out what is happening—but do not let yourself be seen outside on the roof terrace! And report back at once!"

"Yes, sir!"

A moment later the guard came hurrying back and called out, "The elevator's coming down!"

The five persons who had been waiting now surged out of the president's office expectantly. They were in for a nasty shock.

As the elevator door slid open, they saw Captain Said himself. He was clutching his assault rifle, eyes red-rimmed and bleary—his face contorted in an expression of rage and grief!

Ambassador Farouk exclaimed in Arabic—then, remembering the Americans present, switched to English. "What has happened, Captain? Tell us at once! Is His Highness safe?"

The giant bodyguard shook his head. He was struggling to speak and control his emotion. "No!" His voice came out at last in a harsh croak. "Prince Haroun has been kidnapped!"

"*Kidnapped?*" The ambassador's horror was reflected in his face.

Yusef poured out his story—about the helicopter

landing, the blinding spotlight and the gas attack, and how, when the dense fumes finally cleared and he had recovered from being maced, the prince was gone.

Then he began to weep and pound his forehead with his huge fists.

"Wait!" Eric cut in awkwardly. "Carrying on like this won't help Prince Haroun."

"Nothing can help him now!" Ambassador Farouk flung up his hands in despair. "At this moment His Highness is doubtless at the mercy of bloodthirsty fanatics—if indeed he is not already dead!"

"But if he was kidnapped, won't he be held for a ransom?" Alison ventured in a small voice.

"That's right," argued Eric. "Whoever's behind it, if their motive was assassination, they could have already done it."

"So he is being held as a hostage," the ambassador replied.

"Surely you'll hear from them and get a chance to negotiate for the prince's safety," said Alison.

"Maybe soon," Eric added. "If they figure on making a deal, they won't want the police involved. Which means they know they've got to talk fast—before you report the kidnapping."

Farouk's eyes began to light up with a glimmer of hope. "What you say is indeed reasonable." He walked back and forth, plucking nervously at his beard. "Perhaps I should return to our U.N. offices and wait for a message."

"They're normally closed at this time, aren't they?"

"True, but what are you suggesting?" the ambassador frowned.

"That you're more likely to get word right here. The kidnappers could probably see all these top-floor lights from their helicopter. Anyhow, common sense should tell them the prince probably didn't come here alone."

"The best thing to do right now," Alison suggested quietly, "is to ask for God's help and guidance."

"Wise advice, my dear." Ambassador Farouk nodded gravely. "Just what the Holy Koran tells us to do at such a time as this."

The three Arabs prostrated themselves on the floor, facing east toward Mecca and murmuring devoutly in Arabic. The Thorne twins bowed their heads to pray.

What happened next was almost like an instant response to their prayers. The telephone rang in the president's office.

Ambassador Farouk's bearded face jerked up from the floor with a startled, wide-eyed expression. Then the plump diplomat scrambled to his feet and darted into the office. His hand trembled as he picked up the phone.

From what they could hear, Eric and Alison guessed that he was talking to the kidnapper. Despite his nervousness, the portly Arab managed to sound both firm and dignified. Yet when he hung up, the first thing Mr. Farouk did was to pull out a handkerchief and mop his perspiring forehead and fat, glistening cheeks.

"Th-th-they have the prince!" he gulped.

"We know that, sir," Abu Kassim exclaimed anxiously. "But what did they say? What do they want?"

"First, they warn us not to call the police or FBI—or, indeed, say anything at all to the American authorities. Should they find out we have done so, they threaten to kill His Highness at once! Meanwhile, we are to await further instructions. If we follow them, they say the prince will not be harmed. But these instructions will be given not to us—not to the official representative of Hajar—but to Eric and Alison Thorne!"

All eyes immediately turned to the twins.

Eric and Alison looked at each other. What had they gotten themselves into! What would Dad say if he knew? If they agreed to pass on instructions, wouldn't that imply they felt it was OK to deal with criminals or terrorists— and therefore that their government also approved?

"We can't refuse," Alison murmured to her brother. "Not if the prince's safety depends on *us!*"

Eric hesitated. No doubt there was a right moral answer to their dilemma, but this was one of those times when it wasn't all that easy to make a judgment.

He nodded glumly. "Guess you're right. It's up to the Emir, not us. He's the one who'll have to decide whether or not to deal with the kidnappers. All we can do is abide by his decision."

It was now past nine a.m. in the Arab lands on the Persian Gulf. The muezzins, high up on the minarets of all the mosques in Hajar, had long since called the faithful to their morning prayers.

Ambassador Farouk placed an overseas call to the Emir's palace. Presently he emerged from the oil company president's office looking pale and shaken, having spoken directly to the ruler of Hajar.

"His Majesty decrees that we are to obey the kidnapper's orders. In other words, we must say nothing to the police or anyone else until we receive instructions regarding the prince's release."

"What about my brother and me?" Alison spoke up. "Are we supposed to stay close to the phone until we hear from the kidnappers?"

"Yes and no, my dear Miss Thorne. We hope, of course, that you will remain in the New York area until His Highness has been rescued or restored to us. However, this does not mean you must remain confined in your hotel room. The kidnapper said he would notify either myself or some member of our U.N. delegation in advance as to when and how he proposed to transmit instruction to you and your brother."

"All right, Mr. Ambassador," said Eric. "We'll keep in touch."

Neither Eric nor Alison slept very soundly that night. The exciting and upsetting events they had just been through had left them too keyed up to relax. Even though it was two a.m. before they retired, both were up and dressed by eight the next morning.

"When's Jared Custer going to drive you to Westchester to see McKee's journal?" Eric asked.

"I don't exactly know," Alison said. "He's supposed to phone me and arrange the details. Why?"

"Maybe it would be better to go this morning—as soon as possible."

"What if the kidnapper calls and expects us to follow through in a hurry?"

"That could happen," Eric admitted. "It could also happen the call will come this afternoon when you're out. So what's the difference? No use holding your breath till we hear. The point is, the sooner you find out from that journal how people disappear at *El Gezirah*, the better. If we know what happened to Al Ghazali, that might even give us some clue to the prince's kidnapping. Or at the very least it might give us some advantage in dealing with the kidnappers—especially if they don't know we've found out how the disappearing act works."

Alison nodded thoughtfully. "You're right." She glanced at her wristwatch. "It's early, but maybe Jared won't mind. I'll call him right now and see if we can go this morning."

The telephone rang as she got up from her chair. The sudden buzz sent the twins' pulses racing skittishly.

Eric, being nearest, snatched up the phone. The voice on the line tingled his pulse in quite a different way than he had expected. The caller was Persia Palmer!

"Did I wake you up?" she began apologetically.

"No way, I've been up for an hour!" Glancing at Alison, Eric saw her lips twitch in a faint smile—and was instantly annoyed that she could guess who it was so easily from his reaction. "Where'd you go last night?" he went on hastily, deciding to ignore his sister. "My friend and I were worried when we didn't find you."

"Well . . . it's a long story." Suddenly Persia's voice sounded very strange. "Look, could I see you this morning, Eric? There's something I want to tell you, and I think it'll be easier if we—well, if we're talking face to face."

"Sure, great idea. Have you had breakfast?"

"Not yet."

"Neither have I, so what do you—" Eric was about to suggest meeting at the coffee shop that Persia was probably calling from, when he suddenly recalled that it might be wiser to stay close to the hotel in case of any developments. "How about dropping over here to the Stuyvesant Plaza for breakfast with my sister and me?" he said instead.

Persia hesitated, but only for a moment. "OK, I'd like that."

"Half an hour?"

"Fine, I'll be there, Eric!"

He hung up and flashed a questioning glance at Alison. "Hope you won't mind company?"

"Of course not. Your girlfriend, I take it?"

"Persia Palmer."

"Is something up?"

Eric shrugged uneasily. "I don't know. She wants to talk about something. Maybe about that letter for Haroun."

Alison phoned Jared Custer and asked the fashion photographer if he could take her to Westchester that morning, instead of in the afternoon. He agreed and arranged to pick her up at ten o'clock. Then the twins went downstairs to the hotel dining room and waited.

Whatever Persia had on her mind seemed to be serious. To Eric, she looked as bewitching as ever with her emerald green eyes and ringleted red hair, but her manner was subdued. She held back from talking until the waitress in the hotel dining room had taken their orders and brought coffee.

Then she said, "Do you mind telling me if that letter to your friend was . . . any kind of bad news?"

"You could call it that," Eric replied. "In fact it turned out to be *very* bad news. Why?"

"It was bad news for me, too."

"What do you mean?"

Persia seemed to take a deep breath. "You remember I told you the envelope had been slipped under my door?"

Eric nodded, puzzled by the red-haired girl's expression. "So?"

"I was wrong. Whoever left it must have broken into my apartment. He was there when I was talking to you on the phone."

"*What?*" both Eric and Alison exclaimed.

"Right after I hung up," Persia explained, "someone grabbed me from behind and held a pad over my nose. It was soaked in chloroform or ether—some sort of anesthetic. That's the last thing I remember. When I woke up, do you know where I found myself?"

The twins shook their heads, fascinated.

"You'll never guess. I was lying under my own bed."

Eric felt a horrible chill trickle down his spine. "You mean you were . . . right there in your apartment when we came over?"

Persia nodded. "After I passed out, whoever did it must have injected me with some kind of sedative." She rolled up one sleeve to reveal a needle puncture. "I finally came to at about seven o'clock this morning."

Eric gasped. "Have you told the police?"

Persia shook her head. "Not yet. I—I thought I should talk to you first." She gulped and went on, "I don't mean to be nosy, Eric, but—who wrote that letter to your friend?"

"Some people who . . . who mean to harm him. And us."

"Then I think I'd better tell you *everything*."

Alison said gently, "You mean you've been holding something back?"

"Worse than that . . . but I might as well get it over with. I mean, it isn't easy telling you this—admitting I'm a fraud—but I am." Persia paused again, took another deep breath, and plunged on. "I told you I was a freelance news photographer working for *Manhattan* magazine. Well, I'm not. At least not *really*."

Her emerald green eyes met Eric's.

"What do you mean, 'not really'?" he asked. "If you're not a news photographer, what are you?"

"An actress. I was hired to play a part."

11 • A Ghostly Intruder

In her typical, tactful, way, Alison tried to smooth over the awkward shock of Persia's confession. "Well, I guess that explains a few things that puzzled us," she said gently. "Want to tell us about it?"

"No," Persia replied with a wan smile, "but I will, anyway. It was one of the editors at *Manhattan* magazine who hired me. The feature editor, Jay Gibbs, to be exact. He gave me a big song and dance about . . ." she glanced at Alison and cringed. "About how an Arabian prince was going to marry an American girl named Alison Thorne, and his father was giving them this fabulous mansion as a wedding present."

"Oh, no!" Alison said. "I'm only sixteen! How could you think—"

"He didn't say anything about your age," she said. "I thought you looked a little young."

Alison burst out laughing.

"Well," Persia went on, red-faced, "you have to admit it would be a great story, really romantic and everything. Mr. Gibbs said his readers love that kind of stuff."

"Even if that were true," said Eric, "and believe me, it

isn't, why hire an actress to go after the story? Why not a seasoned reporter or magazine writer?"

"Because according to him, there was no way you would talk to the press. The only way to gain your confidence would be to meet you, apparently just by chance, with some off-the-wall idea for a cover story."

The sort of put-up job Alison had sensed all along, Eric thought, with a rueful glance at his sister.

"And the bit about you being a fan of old Victorian mansions and especially *El Gezirah*—that was part of the plan?" Alison inquired.

Persia gave a shamefaced nod. "I'm afraid so. Gibbs thought that would be an easy way for me to get chummy with you in a hurry."

"Pretty smart!" said Eric, unable to keep a tinge of bitterness out of his voice.

Persia reached out to touch his hand. "I'm sorry, Eric," she murmured.

Alison said, "And all that stuff you told us about the architect's grandson—just more window dressing?"

"I guess so. I thought it was on the level—Gibbs spoke as if he'd done a lot of research on the subject. But I guess he just made it up."

"Something tells me we ought to do some research on this guy Jay Gibbs," Eric gritted.

Alison nodded thoughtfully. "It would certainly be interesting to know how he found out about us and *El Gezirah*. Or, for that matter, where Gibbs himself fits into the whole picture. Including last night. But how do you go about it without risking a flood of publicity? If you go and see him, won't that be playing right into his hands?"

Eric tried to think calmly. "I don't see any other way. Do you? Look, suppose we take him by surprise. Persia and I'll just barge in on him without calling ahead for an appointment. Then give him a chance to explain. If he can, fine—but his story'd better be good!"

"Yes . . . I guess that makes sense," Alison agreed slowly, "Provided Persia's willing." She flashed the red-haired girl a questioning glance.

Persia gave a wry shrug. "Of course I'm willing. It's the least I can do."

When the twins and their guest finished breakfast and came out of the hotel dining room, they found Jared Custer waiting on a sofa in the lobby.

Alison introduced him to Persia and Eric. The twins began to smile when they saw Jared comparing them with each other.

Manhattan magazine occupied the eighth and ninth floors of a newish glass-and-steel office building on Third Avenue. Eric and Persia had declined Jared's offer to drop them there, since he and Alison were headed in the opposite direction. Besides, it was only a few blocks from the hotel and made a pleasant ten-minute walk in the autumn sunshine.

They got off the elevator on the eighth floor, only to discover that the editorial receptionist was on nine, so they had to ring for the elevator again to be whisked up to the right place. Only later did Eric realize the significance of this.

"May I help you?" said a glossy young woman at the desk. "We'd like to see Jay Gibbs," said Persia.

"Is Mr. Gibbs expecting you?"

"Not exactly, but I'm doing an assignment for him. Shooting a pictorial feature."

"Your name, please?"

"Persia Palmer."

"And you, sir?" She glanced at Eric.

"He's with me," Persia spoke up. "Part of the assignment."

The receptionist lifted her phone and dialed. "Miss Persia Palmer is here, with a young man," she murmured into the telephone mouthpiece—adding after a moment, "She says she's shooting a photographic assignment for you."

There was a pause. Then the receptionist lowered the phone and looked up at Persia with a puzzled frown. "I'm sorry, but Mr. Gibbs says he doesn't know you."

Persia's cheeks flushed. "Well, I know *him!*"

More conversation ensued back and forth. Finally the receptionist seemed to give up. "Mr. Gibbs still thinks you're mistaken, Miss Palmer, but he'll talk to you and try to clear it up. Go right down that hall, please—third door on the left."

Persia's chin tilted as she set off with a determined air. Eric accompanied her, not quite sure what was going on, but already guessing the outcome.

A tall, balding man with a a fretful expression rose from his desk as they entered. "Miss Palmer?"

"Yes, I'm looking for Jay Gibbs."

"I'm Gibbs."

"What?" Persia's emerald eyes widened as she stared at him incredulously. Suddenly her face turned pinker than ever.

"Miss Palmer," the magazine editor said, "I really do believe there's been some kind of mistake."

"So do I! B-b-but never mind, let's just forget the whole thing!"

Face flaming, Persia whirled and marched out of the office. Eric slipped an arm around her protectively as they passed the curious gaze of the receptionist on their way back to the elevator. Neither spoke till they were out on the street again.

"Oh, what an idiot!" Persia murmured at last. Her chin trembled; she was on the verge of tears.

"Never mind, it could happen to anyone," Eric comforted

her. "I take it he wasn't the 'Jay Gibbs' you expected to see . . . which means you got taken in by some phony."

"Did I ever!"

When they were safely seated in the nearest cafe, Persia poured out the whole story. The phony Mr. Gibbs, it seemed, had phoned and invited her to dinner, explaining that he was looking for a talented young actress to carry out a special assignment for *Manhattan* magazine.

"He said the story could be really dynamite and he was the only one who knew. He didn't want to take any chance of losing a scoop this big, not even to the other editors on the magazine staff."

"So he preferred to meet you outside the office."

"Right."

Eric nodded. "I wondered about that, when I realized you'd never been there before today."

Persia made a helpless gesture. "There isn't much more to tell. He said you and your sister were staying at the Stuyvesant Plaza, and then before we left the restaurant, he paid me a hundred dollars in advance. He said there'd be a lot more when I got the whole story."

"How were you supposed to report to him?"

"Well, he said he didn't want me calling him at the office for fear of someone snooping on the line, so he'd call me."

"And did he?"

"Just once. That was yesterday afternoon before you came to the coffee shop. I told him you two wouldn't let me follow you around and shoot any pictures. But at least you were going to go to Brooklyn with me to see the architect's grandson."

Eric was pensive for a while. Persia watched him with an anxious expression. "I still don't know what this is all about," she said remorsefully, "But I guess it must be pretty serious."

Eric nodded. "Very serious. What'd this phony look like?"

"Oh, a long droopy black mustache, glasses, and a big thick mop of curly hair. Almost like an Afro . . . come to think of it, that sounds like a disguise. Was it?"

"Probably. Did he say where he got your name?"

"Not really. Just that some stage manager or director remembered me from a casting call and recommended me." Persia paused to sip her tea before adding, "Eric, tell me one thing. Why did that crook hire me? What was I supposed to find out *really?*"

Eric shrugged uncomfortably and plowed his fingers through his hair. "That's a tough question to answer, Persia—especially when I'm not supposed to talk at all. The main thing is, a serious crime's been committed—and it's a cinch your phony Mr. Jay Gibbs was in on it. I think he hoped to plant you as an inside spy, so you could keep him posted on every move we made. When that didn't pan out, he used you as a way of getting that letter to us—and making sure we'd take it dead seriously!"

Persia tried hard to smile. "Did the guy have to scare the wits out of me and chloroform me, on top of everything else?"

"I guess that was to make sure you didn't spill the beans too soon. The crime was committed last night, you see, and if you'd talked out of turn, it might've messed up their plans." Eric went on reflectively. "By the way. You're an actress. Here's a question maybe you can answer for me."

"I'll try."

"Ever hear of an actress named Cleopatra St. James? Not very successful, I imagine."

Persia's forehead puckered in a slight frown. "Wait a minute. That name does ring a bell."

"She died in a boating accident a while back."

Persia snapped her fingers. "I remember now! It happened a couple of summers ago, before I came to New York. Someone told me she was out in a little sailboat off Fire Island. A storm came up and it overturned.

111

Apparently this girl had been living on the island under an assumed name. But after she drowned, a relative or boyfriend identified her as Cleo St. James—who was supposed to have disappeared. Whoever told me all this figured it was just a trick."

"What do you mean, a trick?"

"To get publicity. He thinks she intended to turn up with some sensational story about being kidnapped or what-ever. You know—probably hoping some talent scout would spot her on a news broadcast and give her a big part in a show."

"That's interesting," said Eric.

"How so?"

"Cleo St. James was one of the people who was sup-posed to have disappeared inside the McKee Mansion."

Going through the Bronx, the part of New York City north of Manhattan, wasn't so nice. The terrible slum areas looked like the bombed-out ruins of a city hit by an air raid—a wasteland of gutted, abandoned tenements. Someday, Alison reflected soberly, her and Eric's genera-tion would have to figure out how to rebuild such places —and it looked as though they would certainly need God's help!

But Alison enjoyed the ride up into Westchester County. Once beyond the urban sprawl, the scenery became much more attractive. They were now in a green suburban area of upper middle class homes.

On the way, Jared told her how he had come to be a fashion photographer. Alison was surprised to learn that he'd enlisted in the Air Force, intending to win an ap-pointment to the U.S. Air Force Academy and become a pilot. Meanwhile, he was assigned to photographic work and quickly became hooked on everything to do with

112

cameras. Some of his pictures had won him a job on a national news magazine after he'd served his hitch.

"From military airplanes to fashions?" said Alison. "That's quite a jump!"

Jared grinned. "Didn't happen quite that fast. One of my news assignments was to cover a Paris fashion show. The shots turned out sensationally well, so the editor kept assigning me more of the same. Then I began getting bids to shoot layouts for advertising agencies. So finally I turned freelance, and here I am! Or here we are, anyhow."

They had just reached the pleasant community where Jared's parents lived. Their half-timbered Tudor-style house stood on a corner lot in a hilly, tree-shaded neighborhood. Its curving driveway could be entered from either of the two streets that formed the corner.

Jared unlocked the front door and, once inside, invited Alison to sit down. "The journal's in the spare bedroom. I'll go get it. Then we'll have a cup of tea while you read it, OK?"

"OK," she said, and she watched him go upstairs.

She stood in the immaculate, expensively furnished living room. It looked like the kind of place where the furniture was mainly for show, not really for sitting. She was looking at some figurines on a bookshelf when she heard an angry cry from upstairs.

"Jared? What is it?"

When she heard no answer, she went upstairs to find him. She was able to locate him by the sound of his angry voice and of dresser drawers being opened and slammed shut.

"They found the book," he said disgustedly, gesturing to where the old volume lay on the bed. "They went and rummaged through half the place before they did, too—what a mess!"

"Who did?"

"How should I know? Whoever it was that broke into the house looking for it!"

She went to the bed and picked up Murdo McKee's journal, leafing through it, There was no doubt that this was what the burglar had been after. Pages 43 through 47 had been torn out.

Eric strolled back to the Stuyvesant Plaza from the Broadway theatrical district. The day was clouding over, reflecting his own state of mind. He felt deflated. It wasn't bad enough, Haroun being kidnapped. Now it looked as though he wasn't likely to see much more of Persia Palmer. He told himself he should be happy over her good luck. But he wasn't.

He'd walked her home to the coffee shop next to her apartment building, trying to stretch out their time together before returning to the hotel. But one of the waitresses had greeted her with exciting news. Her agent had called not five minutes ago with news of a job!

Persia was all agog and immediately phoned him back. When she hung up, her emerald eyes were wider than Eric had ever seen them. "I've got a part in a soap opera!" she chortled ecstatically to him and the waitress and everyone else within hearing distance.

She'd read for the part more than two weeks ago and had given up hoping to be called. But now, without warning, the producer wanted her at the studio before twelve o'clock!

"Hey, that's wonderful, Persia!" Eric congratulated her, trying to sound enthusiastic.

She kissed him hastily before scampering up to her flat. "I'd better go get ready. Wish me luck!"

So now Eric was on his way back to the hotel. He hoped Alison was having better luck than he was. As he walked along, he noticed a street-corner telephone booth and decided to try phoning Tom Peel again. After all, Mrs. Peel had invited him to call back. She might have heard from her husband.

Eric got the number from Information and dialed. Mrs. Peel answered.

"This is Eric Thorne again," he told her.

"Oh, yes . . ."

Was he imagining things, or did her tight-lipped cautious voice sound a bit more cordial and human than before? Eric felt a twinge of hope.

"You said I might call back to find out if you'd heard from Mr. Peel," he began.

"Yes, I know—and I *have* heard from him. I told him about your call."

"Great! Is there any way I could talk to him?"

"He'll be in touch."

The receiver clicked down at the other end, as abruptly as before.

Eric hung up, feeling almost as before. Almost, but not quite. At least now a fresh glimmer of hope had appeared on the horizon.

At the Stuyvesant Plaza, the desk clerk handed him a yellow slip of paper along with his key. Eric was pleasantly startled. Had that fresh glimmer suddenly turned into a beam of sunshine?

The yellow paper bore a telephone message: *Bristol Bookshop on Fifth Avenue called 10:15—said the book you ordered is in.*

Eric frowned in puzzlement. *What* book? What was this all about? . . . A mistake of some kind? Message delivered to the wrong party?

But no—the note was specifically addressed to Eric Thorne.

He glanced at his watch—11:23. "Know where the Bristol Bookshop is?" he asked the desk clerk.

"Two blocks over on fifth Avenue, then one block north."

It didn't sound too far away. Eric set out at a brisk pace. The bookshop proved to be a large, pleasant one room store crammed with paperbacks and hardcover books in colorful jackets.

"Do you have a book for Eric Thorne?" he inquired.

The woman at the cash register peered under the counter. "Ah, yes . . . here it is." As she pulled it out, Eric saw that the book was circled by a rubber band, holding a piece of white paper with his name and some writing on it. "Looks like someone left a note for you," she added.

She handed the book to Eric. He read the note:

BUYER SAYS TO TELL MR. THORNE
THE COVER TIME IS 2:00 AND
HE'LL NEED GLASSES

12 • The Lady With the Lamp

Eric regarded the note with baffled stare. "I don't get it," he muttered, looking up at the woman clerk.

"I don't, either," she agreed with a smile.

"What's this about the 'buyer'?"

"I suppose it's whoever bought the book."

"You mean the book is all bought and paid for?"

"Apparently so. Here's the receipt." She showed him a cash register tape, which was stuck between the pages of the book.

"Did you make the sale?" Eric asked.

"No, I guess Mr. Chan must have." She turned to a young man with Chinese features who was arranging stock on a nearby table. "Did you sell this, Roy?" she asked him.

"Yes, what about it?" He left his work to join them. "Any problem?"

"Can you tell me what this means?" Eric asked, pointing to the note.

"Not really. That's just what the man said to tell you."

"What man?"

"The guy who bought it. He said you'd be in sometime

117

today to pick up the book and asked me to give you that message. He said you'd understand what it meant."

"What did he look like?"

Chan didn't even have to stop and jog his memory. "A red-haired fella with an eyepatch."

Eyepatch! That had to mean Tom Peel. So this was his way of getting in touch!

"OK, thanks. I've got it now," Eric said with a vague smile.

The two sales clerks watched curiously as he picked up the book and walked out of the store.

It was not quite 12:30 when Alison arrived back at the Stuyvesant Plaza. She found Eric poring over the note and the book while he munched on the last of three hamburgers he'd brought back to the hotel.

"Actually this one was for you," he apologized. "But I wasn't sure how soon you'd be back, and I didn't want it to go to waste."

Alison grinned. "Jared and I had lunch before he dropped me off."

She quickly reported what had happened at his parents' house. Then Eric filled her in on his own morning's adventures.

Alison was immediately intrigued. "May I see the book?"

It was titled, THIS IS NEW YORK! *A Tourist Guide to the Island of Manhattan.* She flipped through its pages, which were filled with both pictures and text. "Have you figured out yet what it means?"

Eric hesitated, as if afraid she might make fun of his solution. "Well, I've come up with one possible answer . . . but you may think it's pretty far out."

"Try me."

"Well, on the cover is this picture of New York harbor

with the Statue of Liberty in the foreground. So when he says *Cover time is 2:00,* he means, 'Be out at the Statue of Liberty at two o'clock.' And *he'll need glasses* means we'll need binoculars. In other words, Peel intends to signal us in some way, and we'll only be able to see his signal through field glasses."

"Hmm." Alison looked both impressed and dubious. "That's pretty ingenious, Eric, I'll have to admit. I can't think of any other interpretation that would fit both parts of the message. But why on earth would Peel have to communicate with us in such a roundabout way?"

"Because he's in fear of his life, that's why! Somebody tried to run him down with a truck, remember? They scared him so badly that now he's pretending to be out of the country."

"Eric, that's positively brilliant!"

"You want to give it a try?"

"What have we got to lose? Besides, I've always wanted to visit the Statue of Liberty!"

The air was filled with tangy sea smells and the mewing of gulls. The water was thronged with vessels moving in and out of New York harbor. The twins had caught the ferry to Liberty Island in Battery Park, at the southern tip of Manhattan. Now after its brief voyage across the bay, the boat was moving in to dock at the tiny island that bore France's 225-ton gift to the first republic of the New World . . . the Lady With the Lamp.

Both Alison and Eric felt a peculiar thrill of emotion during their walk from the island pier toward the building that formed the statue's base. A chill of patriotic pride prickled their scalps and they each felt a lump rising in their throats as they stared up at the towering green copper figure.

"Quite a sight, isn't she?" murmured Eric.

"She's really something!" Alison agreed, hating herself for lacking grander words at such a moment.

An elevator took them up to the slender staircase that sightseers ascended, single file. It spiraled upward inside the statue's steel framework, from the hem of Miss Liberty's gown all the way to her crown.

As they reached the windowed room at the top, from which visitors could look out over the harbor, the twins suddenly realized the crucial importance of timing. The constant flow of people resulted in a silent pressure to "take your look and move on."

So far they had managed remarkably well. Alison's watch showed a little more than five minutes to go before two o'clock. They stalled and dawdled near the back wall, letting others crowd past them. Then, with two minutes left before two, the twins got back in line, made their way to the windows, and looked out.

The view was breathtaking! To their left across the water, Manhattan with its cluster of skyscrapers . . . Governors Island . . . Brooklyn . . . and far to the south, on their right, the Verrazano Bridge spanning the Narrows.

All around, the blue expanse of the Upper Bay was dotted with toy ships. Eric hastily focused his binoculars and began picking out the vessels . . . a sleek Coast Guard cutter, three or four blackened, rusty oceangoing freighters, a graceful sailing yacht, a tug herding a big cruise liner into port, a Navy destroyer, several small fishing craft . . .

Suddenly his pulse quickened as his glasses fixed on a small cabin cruiser. A man was visible in the cockpit—*a man with an eyepatch!*

The man mounted the fly bridge above the cabin and held up a sign aimed toward the Statue of Liberty . . . a large white square of cardboard with black lettering on it!

Eric jabbed Alison with his elbow, handed her the binoculars, and pointed out what he had just seen.

She peered through the glasses. Her face took on an expression of growing excitement as she, in turn, read the lettering on the homemade sign:

P 46
L 9
W 1-2-3

The twins puzzled over its meaning all the way back on the ferry from Liberty Island to the Battery, and then by taxi up through the honking, brake-screeching mid-afternoon traffic to the Stuyvesant Plaza.

Their lengthy discussion got them exactly nowhere. By the time they reached their hotel room at a quarter past three, they were almost ready to give up.

Alison paused in the center of their sitting room to stretch her neck back wearily. Right now she needed to sit down and relax. She reached out to pick up the tourist guidebook, THIS IS NEW YORK!, from the easy chair where Eric had tossed it just before they left the hotel. Oh, what a pleasure it would be to fling herself down on that cushioned upholstery and get her feet up on a hassock!

Instead, Alison suddenly straightened up, as if someone had jabbed her with a needle. "Eric!" she gasped. "I think I've got it!"

He stared at her, half hopefully, half skeptically, "OK, explain it to me."

"P means page—L means line—and W means words! And the book is obviously this same one he left for you at the store!"

Eric's eyes widened like the sun coming out from behind a cloud. "I'll bet you really have got it!"

Excitedly they leafed through the book to page 46. It bore a picture of the famous facade of the New York Public

Library with its two stone lions guarding the steps up to the entrance. And the first three words on line 9 of the text were *The library lions.*

"Oh!" said Alison in a hushed voice. "You realize what that must refer to?"

"I'll say I do! Those carved wooden lions in the library at *El Gezirah!* They must have something to do with the secret of all those disappearances!"

"Right! . . . But what?"

There was silence for a few moments.

Then Alison said, "I'm just guessing, but maybe there's a hollow space in one of those lions where something's hidden. Maybe written information, like whatever was on those pages that were torn out of Murdo McKee's journal."

Eric nodded thoughtfully. "Or maybe something's hidden *under* one of the lions. What do you think, Allie?"

"I think we ought to go back to the mansion for another look. And the sooner the better!"

The telephone rang, sending both their heartbeats racing.

Eric snatched it up. "Hello?"

"Perhaps you have already recognized my voice, eh? I am Ambassador Farouk, I have just received a call from— from the party we dealing with, in connection with what happened last night."

"I understand, sir," Eric responded with a glance at Alison, who was listening transfixed. "Is there some new development?"

"Yes, and very important! The caller indicated that all would be well, following payment of a ransom."

"A ransom! Did they say how much, or how it would be paid?"

"Not yet. That is where you and your sister can be of help. He said he would contact you shortly and would explain all the necessary details at that time. He also indicated that he wished you two to handle the actual payment of the ransom, and the release of the—of their prisoner." Farouk paused as if awaiting some comment, then went on anxiously, "You are willing to do so, I hope?"

It was Eric's turn to pause. "Yes, sir. I guess so . . . now that we've gone this far. As long as the conditions sound reasonable and on the level."

"I have already spoken to the Emir Nasreddin before calling you," Ambassador Farouk put in hastily. "He is willing to accept almost any terms, providing they are not political. His royal government will not bow to threats from rebels or terrorists. But financially speaking, no price would be too high to ensure his son's safe return."

"I understand, sir. So what's the next step for my sister and me? Just stand by and wait for his call?"

"Exactly. That seems to be the proper course. You will let us know at once when you hear from him, I trust?"

"Yes, sir. You can count on that!"

After cutting short the envoy's profuse thanks, Eric hung up and told Alison the gist of their conversation. Both were stricken with doubts about proceeding, but the course of events seemed to have taken that decision out of their hands.

Less than ten minutes later, the telephone rang again. When Eric answered, a man spoke, sounding muffled and far away, as if he were using some sort of filter to disguise his voice.

"You know why I'm calling?"

"I know," Eric said curtly.

"The price is the Mullagar Ruby."

"Mullagar Ruby?" Eric echoed, flashing a puzzled frown at Alison.

"That's the ruby the Emir bought at auction last week!" she hissed back. "It's worth two million dollars! Ed Bancroft mentioned it when he first told us about meeting Haroun—remember?"

"Oh—yes!" Eric said, both to her and into the phone.

"The payment will be made tonight," the caller went on. "Follow these instructions carefully. As soon as possible, start out from the hotel in the royal limousine. Time is of the essence. Bring the ruby with you. Drive north on Park Avenue."

"I understand. Then what?"

There was no answer. The caller had just hung up.

Eric slammed his own telephone back into its cradle with a furious expression.

"I don't like it, either." Alison agreed after hearing his report. "But the man did say 'as soon as possible.' You'd better call the ambassador right back."

Farouk sounded overjoyed when he heard the news. "There will be no difficulty about the ruby. It is now at the jeweler's, being set in a ring for one of the Emir's wives. I shall have Captain Said pick it up at once and then drive to your hotel."

"You understand, sir, the people we're dealing with may not be trustworthy," Eric cautioned. "They've already pulled one trick when they captured Prince Haroun. How can we be sure they won't try to stage an armed holdup right in broad daylight, if they know we have a two-million dollar ruby with us in the car?"

"I think we may depend on Captain Said to deal with that eventuality," said the ambassador. "Go with God, my son—may He crown with success our efforts to save his Highness!"

This time Eric hung up silently praying his own prayer.

Everything had gone with remarkable speed and smoothness. Less than half an hour after Eric transmitted the kidnapper's instructions to Ambassador Farouk, the royal limousine had drawn up in front of the hotel and the

Thorne twins had hastily climbed in. Now they were cruising north on Park Avenue as directed. The partition between driver and passengers had been lowered, so that the twins could converse directly with Yusef without using the voice tube. The huge Arab was carrying the precious ruby ring in one pocket of his uniform and had a machine pistol lying in quick reach on the front seat beside him.

They had just crossed 74th Street when the car's telephone purred. Alison answered.

"Miss Thorne?"

"Speaking."

"Listen carefully. Have your driver swing over west to the Metropolitan Museum of Art. Go inside and look for the room where arms and armor are displayed. It's on the main floor. It contains mounted figures of knights on horseback. A guard can direct you, or you can pick up a floor plan of the museum from the counter in the—"

"I know where it is. We've been there before," Alison interrupted impatiently.

"Good. Once you're in that room, look for a display case containing old flintlock pistols. Reach underneath that display case and you'll find a note taped to the bottom. Read what it says."

There was a click as the caller hung up abruptly.

Within minutes, the royal limousine pulled up in front of the imposing classical-columned facade of the museum, which was located on Fifth Avenue, on the green edge of Central Park. Eric and Alison jumped out of the car and went hurrying up the broad marble steps.

"Not much time left before closing," the attendant warned as they paid their admission.

"That's OK—we probably won't be here long," Eric replied.

They crossed the great hall and followed a corridor running alongside the main staircase to a room containing a gorgeous display of medieval art. Here they turned right

125

and eventually came to the room containing arms and armor.

At any other time, the twins' eyes would have been eagerly scanning the colorful art treasures and fascinating weapons on exhibit all around them. But at this moment they had only one thought in mind.

Alison quickly found the display case, and as she ran her fingers underneath it, she soon found the taped note. It contained a telephone number and a message:

CALL IMMEDIATELY!
IF LINE IS BUSY, KEEP TRYING!

"Probably the number of a public phone booth," Eric guessed.

They found a pay telephone in the museum lobby. Eric dialed the number and the receiver at the other end was lifted instantly, even before the first ring was completed.

"Who's calling?" said a man's voice.

"Eric Thorne."

"You got a map of the New York area?"

"I'm sure the driver does."

"If he doesn't, tell him to get one. Got a pencil there?"

"Yes." Eric groped in his pocket. Alison offered a scrap of paper from her bag.

"Write down these directions. Take the Triborough Bridge east into Queens. That'll put you on Grand Central Parkway. From there get on Northern Boulevard or 25A. Follow that out along the North Shore of Long Island. About 25 miles, and you'll go down a steep hill leading into a town called Cold Spring Harbor. Got all that?"

"I think so." Eric repeated what he had been told.

"At the bottom of the hill, you'll find a fish hatchery on your right and a biological lab on your left. Pull off the road and park at the hatchery. . . ."

The instructions continued.

A few minutes later the Thorne twins emerged from the museum. Captain Said was still waiting for them in the royal limousine. Its diplomatic license plates insured its immunity to traffic ticketing. The twins took their places in the back seat, and Eric relayed the directions he had just received to their Arab companion.

"Can you follow them?"

Yusef nodded. "There will be no problem."

He started the engine and steered out into the stream of traffic, swinging left at the next traffic light in order to turn northward again later on the Franklin D. Roosevelt Drive and head for the Triborough Bridge.

"Just one thing I don't understand," Alison mused aloud.

"What's that?" asked Eric.

"Why did the kidnappers send us into the museum to make that call? They'd already contacted us once over the car telephone. Why not give us directions the same way?"

"Remember, this is a mobile telephone," Eric pointed out. "It transmits calls by radio, not over a wire."

Alison frowned. "So?"

"So that means the police can monitor any calls we get this way. They don't need a bug or a phone tap. By having us call that number from a phone booth in the museum, the kidnappers were making sure the police wouldn't be listening in when they gave us directions."

"I see what you mean," Alison said thoughtfully. "I guess that must be the reason."

All the same, she wasn't totally convinced. Something at the back of her mind still bothered her.

13 • A Scream in the Dark

The Friday afternoon commuter traffic pouring out of New York City onto Long Island was bumper to bumper. As a result, it was long after dark when the royal limousine came gliding down the hill toward the fish hatchery outside of Cold Spring Harbor.

They parked on the hatchery grounds, and the twins got out, armed with a flashlight provided by Yusef. Behind the hatchery stood a white frame church, just as the kidnapper had said. It was located near the shore of a lake, with woods all around. He had also said there were two tiffany stained glass windows in the back wall of the church.

"Here they are," Eric muttered, shining the flashlight beam from one to the other. "Now—thirty paces from the window nearest the lake, going away from the road." He paced them off, trying to take average steps of equal length.

Twenty-eight steps (which Eric thought was close enough to thirty) brought him to an oak tree such as the kidnapper had mentioned. He shone the flashlight around the base of its trunk.

Sure enough, there was a note taped to the tree! It said:

DRIVE ON INTO COLD SPRING HARBOR.
WAIT FOR A CALL IN THE PHONE BOOTH
NEAR THE FIREHOUSE ON MAIN STREET.

Alison sighed. "Here we go again."

Cold Spring Harbor was an old-time whaling port, with its buildings stretching along the waterfront. Judging from the shops and window signs, it had grown arty and fashionable. Yusef parked near the telephone booth referred to in the note.

Less than five minutes later, they heard the phone ring.

"Someone must be watching us!" Eric exclaimed as he leaped out of the car to answer it.

He picked up the receiver. "Hello?"

"Listen carefully," said a voice. Eric couldn't be sure whether or not it was the same one he'd heard back at the museum. "Turn around and drive back to New York. Take the Lincoln Tunnel over to New Jersey. Drive to the town of Summit. Got that?"

"I heard you. Summit."

"Find the railroad station. It'll be locked up, but wait outside at the rear of the station. That's the side facing toward the business district. You'll see a phone booth on the right of the doors leading into the station, near the steps going down to the platform. Wait there for a call."

"Wait a minute yourself!" Eric burst out angrily. "What kind of a runaround are you giv-"

"You heard my instructions," the voice cut in coldly. "If you want to see your friend again, follow them. And no tricks! Understand? Any sign of funny business, and the ambassador will get one of the prince's ears in the mail!"

The line went dead as the caller hung up.

Eric returned to the car with a cold feeling in the pit of his stomach. He reported to Alison and Captain Said what

129

the caller had told him. "Let's just hope they're not playing games!" he fumed.

"Be patient," the burly, mustachioed Arab counseled. "No doubt they are watching us carefully to make sure we are not under police surveillance. In a way all this may even be a hopeful sign. It indicates their intentions are serious. Also, it is only natural that they should prefer the exchange of the prisoner and the ransom to take place after dark, and as late as possible."

The Thorne twins took what comfort they could from Yusef's line of reasoning during the long drive back into the city. Once again traffic was heavy—this time with entertainment seekers heading into Manhattan for a night on the town. It was 8:45 by the time the limousine nosed into one of the white-tiled passageways of the Lincoln Tunnel, burrowed deep under the Hudson River. When they reached Summit, the time was nearing 9:30.

The town was quiet as they drew up outside the railroad station, but aside from the street lamps, lights still shone from several restaurants and shop windows. A ten-minute wait ensued. Then the silence was broken by a sudden loud ringing from the phone booth. Eric was out of the car like a flash, snatching up the receiver.

When he answered, a voice said, "Reach under the phone shelf. You'll find a paper taped there, like that note taped under the gun case at the museum."

Eric felt with his hand. "OK, I've got it."

The voice gave him elaborate instructions.

Two pairs of eyes watched from the limousine. When Eric returned to the car, Alison said tensely, "What now?"

"We have to go to some wooded park near here, called the Watchung Reservation."

"Where is that?" asked Yusef.

Eric handed him the paper, which bore a crude map drawn in pencil. "I'll give you the rest of the instructions on the way. Let's get going!"

Their route was a wide but poorly lit road running along the foot of the hill on which the town of Summit was situated. After a time they turned off onto a narrower, winding road that led into the reservation.

"I do not like this," muttered Yusef, half to himself. His fierce, black-mustached face was eerily illuminated by the glow of the instrument panel.

"Neither do I," said Eric. "We've no assurance at all the kidnappers are on the level."

When the huge Arab made no comment, he added, "Still want to go through with it?"

Yusef shrugged uneasily. "We have no choice. It is the Emir's will."

Woods hemmed them in on either side. Dimly through the trees on their right, they could see the glimmering, moon-dappled waters on a lake. Except for moonlight, the park was unlighted. Eric's informant had told him it closed at sunset.

Farther on, the trees began to thin out, revealing a more open space of parkland ahead. Here they took a turnoff road to the right, which continued to skirt the lake. As they reached a stucco pavilion, the limousine came to a halt.

"Give me the ruby," said Eric.

Yusef withdrew a small box from his pocket. It contained the ring on which the ruby had been mounted. He handed the box to Eric, who opened the car door and stepped out of the limousine. Eric made a sweeping glance in all directions, but could see little.

The pavilion, which looked as if it might once have been a bathhouse, consisted of two smaller buildings joined by a single roof but with a passageway running between them. One of the two buildings had a counter and apparently served as a refreshment stand, but was now shuttered for the night.

Eric placed the ring box on the counter and returned to the limousine, which glided slowly on.

Their headlights carved a yellow path through the darkness ahead. The road now appeared to border a playground on their left. About a hundred feet past the pavilion, Yusef swung the car sharply off the road, then braked to a halt and switched off their lights.

A heavy silence pervaded the night, broken only by a faint drowsy chirping of crickets. All three occupants of the limousine peered intently toward the pavilion. Even in the moonlight, it was only dimly visible.

A sudden shot rang out, galvanizing them into action. Then another and another, followed by a scream!

"Help! Help me!" cried a muffled voice.

"Is that Haroun?" Eric exclaimed. By now, he and the chauffeur-bodyguard were out of the car.

"We shall soon find out!" returned Captain Said. He was clutching the machine pistol in one hand and a flashlight in the other.

They ran toward the sounds, which appeared to be coming not from the pavilion, but from the opposite direction. The shots had ceased, but in the pitch darkness they could hear angry cries and scuffling, as if a violent struggle was taking place.

Just ahead loomed another building, fringed with trees and brush. Strangely, no figures could be seen, even though the sounds grew louder as they approached. Yusef played his flashlight back and forth, trying to locate the source.

"There! In that clump of bushes!" Eric pointed.

A metallic, boxlike object gleamed among the shrubbery. As the flashlight focused on it, Eric gave a cry of angry frustration. "It's a tape recorder!"

The output had been turned up to full volume. *They had been hearing voices and sound effects on tape!*

With a furious oath in Arabic, the giant captain stopped short, wheeled around, and headed back toward the limousine. Eric paused long enough to snatch up the recorder, switch it off, and follow as fast as his long legs would carry him.

Alison was standing beside the car. "What happened?" she asked.

Eric held up the tape recorder. "We've been tricked again."

"Oh, no!" she said in anger, but suddenly she stopped and pointed to the pavilion. "Eric, the ruby!"

Yusef and Eric ran toward the building. Their fears were soon realized. The box containing the ruby ring had vanished from the refreshment counter. But of Prince Haroun there was no sign!

"Where is he?" Yusef bellowed into the darkness. "Where is my royal master?"

His yell echoed through the wooded park.

There was no response.

The Arab captain was shaking with rage. Eric knew his shouts were useless. By now, whoever had snatched the ransom was hurriedly sneaking farther and farther away through the pitch-black woodlands. Gently Eric took Yusef by the arm and urged him back toward the limousine.

"Shouting won't help. It'll only bring the police if there are any around."

As they rejoined Alison, Eric fancied he heard the faint *vroom* of a car engine starting up and fading in the distance. The sound was too vague even to be sure of the direction, but if it came from the ransom-taker's car, his likeliest way of escape would be via Route 22, a busy multilane highway running along the opposite side of the reservation from the side on which they themselves had approached.

Whatever his getaway route, the bottom line remained the same. The $2,000,000 ruby was gone and Prince Haroun was still missing. A grim, baffled silence settled over the unhappy trio in the limousine.

"May I make a suggestion?" Alison ventured timidly.

Captain Said shrugged his massive shoulders. "Why not?"

"Before Eric and I got that phone call about the ransom, we'd worked out a theory."

"What sort of theory?"

"That we might find a clue to Al Ghazali's disappearance in the library at *El Gezirah*. If we could, it might help us track down Prince Haroun's kidnapper's."

Between them, the twins told their Arab companion about their trip to the Statue of Liberty that afternoon, and the chain of reasoning that had pointed them toward the library lions.

"It is worth a try," Yusef grunted after considering for a few moments. "Anything is worth a try at this point. What other hope have we?"

It was past eleven as the royal limousine once again glided up the curving drive toward the splendid Moorish-style mansion. Lights glowed at the archway, and also from several of the ground floor windows.

Al Ghazali's rented car was still standing where they had first seen it. The entrance gate was unlocked, and the three went through into the flagstoned courtyard with its nymph- and dolphin-ornamented fountain.

In returning to the mansion at this late hour of the night, the twins were relying on the word of the lawyer for the McKee estate, G. Humphrey Ward, that the real estate agency would maintain a round-the-clock vigil at *El Gezirah* in hopes that the missing football star might yet turn up safely of his own accord. As it turned out, the agent on duty was the horn-rimmed, pipe-smoking Fred Jessup, whom they had already met on their first visit to the mansion.

He opened the front door to greet them before they could ring the bell. "Well! This is a surprise!" Jessup spoke with a salesman's typical heartiness, but his eyes darted inquisitively from one to the other of the trio. He also noticed the machine pistol clutched in Yusef's right hand. "Has something happened?"

"We decided to search the house a little more," Alison replied vaguely.

Jessup's sandy eyebrows rose, and he glanced pointedly at his wristwatch. "When it's going on midnight?"

"You've no objection, have you?" Eric responded coolly.

"Oh, no! No, of course not. I just wondered."

An electric coffee maker was going in the sitting room just off the foyer. Evidently the real estate salesman had been comfortably ensconced on the sofa, reading a paperback novel and keeping himself awake with coffee.

"Like some?" Jessup offered.

All three declined, but Alison asked with genuine curiosity, "Has *El Gezirah* always had electricity?"

"Oh, yes," the real estate man nodded. "It was built in the 1890's soon after electric lighting came into fashion. At first Murdo McKee had his own steam-powered generator, but once electric power became generally available, of course, he switched over to the public utility."

Inwardly Eric was squirming with impatience. "Well, we'll go and look around then, if you don't mind," he said, cutting short the conversation.

"By all means. Can I help?" asked Jessup.

"Uh, no thanks. Not yet, anyhow. If we have any problems, we'll call."

The three headed for the library.

The lions, which were carved out of wood and gaudily painted, stood on either side of a massive stone fireplace. Elsewhere, the four walls were lined with high shelves of books.

"Oh, goodness," murmured Alison, suddenly awed by the gravity of the task they had set themselves and fearful that the whole idea might prove a false scent. "Where do we begin?"

"You take one lion, and I'll take the other!" Eric said

energetically. Yusef watched in frowning silence as the twins began running their hands and eyes with slow, careful attention over their respective wooden figures.

It was immediately apparent that nothing could be hidden *under* the carved beasts. Both were immovable, their paws evidently bolted to the floor. Nor was there any sign of a crack or aperture on either, which might indicate a concealed opening. Each bore an ornate painted harness that added to their look of carousel ancestry.

Eric and Alison traded places to double-check each other's inspections.

"Look!" Alison murmured softly. "Here's something different."

On the front of each lion's harness was a painted disk, bearing the same coat-of-arms they had seen on the wrought iron entrance gate and at various places inside the mansion. Presumably this was the coat-of-arms of the McKee family. But where the heraldic crest on one lion included a knight's mailed gauntlet holding a sword, on the other lion the mailed fist was holding a large key!

"Hmm. Maybe it's a pun on the name 'McKee'—as if it were spelled M-c-K-E-Y," suggested Eric.

"Maybe." Alison looked dubious. "But why just on one?"

There was a long silence. Then Eric suddenly blurted, "Wait a minute! That's not the only difference!"

"What else?"

"The eyes! On this one with the key, the eyeballs *bulge* more—in fact they almost look as if they've been attached, instead of carved out. At least this right eyeball does!"

As he spoke, Eric reached out and grasped the feature in question between his thumb and forefinger, to see if it showed any sign of looseness.

To his amazement, the eyeball turned. They heard a faint creaking noise. Captain Said let out a startled bellow.

The bookcase to the right of the fireplace was swinging out from the wall!

14 • *The Secret of El Gezirah*

As the bookcase opened, a light flashed on behind it.

"There's a stairway!" Alison gasped. A flight of stone steps slanted downward.

The twins surged toward the wall opening, eager to explore the secret passage. But the huge Arab barred their way.

"Let me go first," Yusef cautioned. "We do not yet know where this leads."

Ducking his head, he strode into the wall opening and started down the steps, holding his burp gun at the ready. The twins followed single file, peering anxiously over the chauffeur-bodyguard's massive shoulders to see what lay below.

At the foot of the stops stood a metal door. In its center they could see something small and round.

"A push button," Yusef said, as if in reply to their unspoken question.

"Try it!" Eric urged.

Yusef pressed the button with his big forefinger. Slowly the metal door began to slide open moving into a wall slot.

At the same time, Eric heard a gentle creaking above and behind him. The bookcase was closing!

With a yelp of alarm, he dashed back up the steps and tried to hold it open with his shoulder. No use—the pressure was too great to resist!

Casting about desperately, Eric saw a small four-legged stool standing in front of the next bookcase. He reached out, grabbed it, and used it to jam open the swinging portal. There was a muffled screech and groan, as of grinding gears, but the stool held without crushing or breaking. The bookcase ceased to close.

Eric heaved a sigh of relief, then dashed back downstairs to rejoin his companions.

By this time, the sliding metal door at the foot of the steps was wide open. Yusef and Alison gave glad cries as they saw two figures facing them from beyond the door.

One was Prince Haroun! The other was a tall, muscular man whom Alison instantly recognized as the star running back of the Chicago Bears, Al Ghazali! He was badly in need a shave, but he looked unharmed.

Both Captain Said and his royal master began spouting Arabic and rushed toward each other joyfully. The bodyguard sank to one knee and kissed Haroun's hand. The prince smiled and held out his other hand to squeeze one of Alison's. In the next few moments both Al Ghazali and Eric joined in the happy celebration.

"His Highness kept promising me you'd get us out of here!" Al Ghazali told the twins, after hugging Alison and shaking hands warmly with Eric and Yusef.

Excited explanations poured out. Al Ghazali told about the mysterious phone call he had received soon after arriving at the mansion and meeting the real estate man, Fred Jessup.

"Who was the caller?" Eric asked.

"Search me. It was a stranger's voice. He said he'd heard I was going to look over the mansion for some prospective buyer, so he was calling to warn me that the house had a secret underground room that contained something very unpleasant—something the Ludlow Real Estate Agency didn't want me to find out."

"What was it?" exclaimed Alison with a look of wide-eyed interest.

"He wouldn't tell me—just advised me to find out for myself when none of the real estate people were around. So I told Jessup I'd like some more time to check out the condition of the house and asked him to come back later. When he left, I did just what the caller told me to do—turn the right eye of the right-hand lion in the library. The bookcase opened and I saw that flight of stone steps. So I went down to the metal door, pushed the button, and the door slid open. The I saw this room and walked in like a dope to look around, and *wham!* the door slid shut and I was trapped in here—by the way, how did you people keep that metal door from closing?"

The twins and Yusef looked surprised.

"We didn't even know it was *supposed* to close." Alison confessed.

"I'll bet I can guess, though," said Eric. "Pushing that button not only opens the downstairs door, it also makes the bookcase swing back into the wall. And when the book-case closes, that must hit a switch that closes the downstairs door. Only I've got the bookcase propped open—so it *can't* trigger the door switch."

Ghazali nodded thoughtfully. "That makes sense. Smart thinking, Eric!"

After being trapped, the football star said he had shouted and pounded many times during the hours that followed, but apparently had not been able to make himself heard in other parts of the house. Nor had anyone come to check on him until Prince Haroun was brought into the room, blindfolded and with his hands tied behind his back.

Haroun told how he had been kidnapped from the Crescent Oil skyscraper by two armed men.

"Who were they, Your Highness?" Captain Said inquired eagerly. "Hajarite rebels?"

The prince shook his head. "No. They looked and acted more like American gangsters in the movies."

The chopper, he related, had landed in open country somewhere outside New York City, where he was tied, blindfolded, and taken to the mansion by car.

"Didn't they give you any hint of who was masterminding all this?" asked Eric.

Haroun shrugged. "One of the men in the car, I think, was the boss. The others called him 'Mister Barton.' And there was a sly-looking baldheaded chap with him called 'Monk.' That is all I can tell you."

The twins looked around curiously. The secret underground chamber was actually a three-room apartment consisting of a comfortably furnished living room/bedroom, a small bathroom, and a kitchenette that was well-stocked with canned goods.

"So this is where old Murdo McKee used to hole up when he didn't want anyone to find him," mused Eric. "Must've come in handy when his business affairs got ticklish, or creditors were after him."

"That servant and the workman who disappeared must have stumbled on the secret," Alison guessed. "When they went down to see where the steps behind the bookcase led, they got trapped the same way Mr. Ghazali did."

"Then when Murdo McKee came home and rescued them," Eric added, "he probably bribed them not to give away his secret."

"Which reminds me," Alison exclaimed. "Wasn't there any real estate agent on duty when your kidnappers brought you here, Haroun?"

"I have no idea," the prince shrugged. "As I told you, I was blindfolded."

"But Ludlow Realty promised to have someone here all the time! Surely that person would have said something or called the police when he saw the kidnappers bring you here. For that matter, how did they even get inside the mansion?"

Haroun frowned and shook his head. "I do not know. I have wondered that myself. At the time, of course, I did not realize where I was being taken. I only found out I was here after Al Ghazali untied me and took off my blindfold."

The twins turned to the football player, but he too could offer no further explanation. "I didn't even see who brought him," Ghazali said. "I was asleep. They made enough noise to wake me up, but by then—"

He broke off at a sudden cry from Alison. The the light above the stone steps had just gone out.

And now the metal door was starting to slide shut!

Captain Said, who was nearest, dashed to the doorway to stop it from closing. But he was too late! Even his powerful hands and arms could not slow the movement of the metal door. In desperation, he thrust the stock of his machine pistol into the narrow opening. A grating, crunching nose ensued as the mechanism ground to a halt.

The door was still open, but not nearly enough to let someone slip through. The five persons in the underground apartment looked at each other in dismay.

"What happened?" Prince Haroun exclaimed.

"The stool I used to block open the bookcase must've slipped out of place," Eric guessed. "If my theory's right, the closing of the bookcase is what makes this downstairs door slide shut—and also switches off the stairway light, I imagine."

"What about the real estate people?" Al Ghazali spoke up. "Your sister said someone's supposed to be on duty here all the time. Did you see anyone when you arrived?"

"Yes, the same agent you talked to—Fred Jessup. He wasn't with us in the library when we turned the lion's eye, but maybe he can hear us through this crack in the door."

Eric put his face close to the narrow opening and began to shout. *"Mr. Jessup! . . . Hey, Mr. Jessup! Can you hear me?!"*

Yusef added his mighty baritone bellow to the outcry.

Presently Jessup's voice came back, muffled and faint. *"I can hear you, but I can't see you! Where are you?"*

Eric countered, *"Are you in the library?"*

"Yes!"

"Can you see those two wooden lions?"

"Yes!"

"Turn the right eye of the right-hand lion!"

"What? I—I don't understand!"

"Turn the right eye of the right-hand lion!" Eric repeated loudly.

"Oh—yes. . . . Now I see!"

The light above the stone steps suddenly went on again, and they could hear a faint creak as the bookcase swung open. The trapped group heaved sighs of relief.

With his face to the door opening, Eric saw the tweed-jacketed figure of Fred Jessup starting downstairs.

"Wait!" Eric shouted. *"Use that stool to block open the bookcase!"*

"Oh, hmmm, right! Of course!"

Jessup turned back toward the library. A few moments later, Eric saw him start downstairs again. When the agent reached the foot of the stone steps, Eric went on:

"Now press that button you see on the door."

"OK."

The metal door began sliding open. Almost in the same instant, Jessup was shoved aside. Two figures could be seen behind him. One was a swarthy young man in a flashy checked suit, the other baldheaded and somewhat older.

There appeared to be others coming down the stone

steps; but Eric and Alison weren't looking at them. Each of the two men now entering the doorway was holding a gun!

"Turn around, all of you!" the younger man barked. "Then get back against that wall—with your hands up high!"

Captain Said had no chance to retrieve his machine pistol from the doorway or try for a fast draw. Eric halfway expected the huge Arab to explode with anger—perhaps even risk a desperate hand-to-hand struggle, which could only have ended in a fatal burst of gunfire. But Yusef was too much of a professional fighting man to indulge in such foolishness. His face froze into a cold, deadly mask as he obeyed the gunman's instructions. Turning like the others, he moved back toward the wall.

One of the gunmen quickly relieved him of his holstered revolver. Then all five were permitted to turn around.

Eric gasped as he saw three persons who had entered the underground room behind the gunmen. One was Fred Jessup. Another was the Hajarite diplomatic aide, Abu Kassim. The third was a well-dressed man, handsome but hard-faced, with a gold tooth gleaming in his mouth as he chuckled at the captives. From the way he stepped forward, he was clearly in charge of whatever was happening.

Prince Haroun exclaimed furiously in Arabic on seeing the diplomatic aide. Kassim replied in the same language with a taunting smile.

"From now on speak English!" rasped the gold-toothed man.

"But of course, Mr. Barton," Kassim apologized. "I was merely telling the young man that his father's reign as Emir will soon be over, and he can no longer expect to be treated as a pampered prince."

Barton chuckled again. "We'll get around to that, don't worry. First I gotta do some thinking. These two Thorne brats are too smart for their own good. They've been a problem all along, but now that they've found this under-ground room, they've really loused up everything! Looks like there's gonna hafta be a slight change of plans."

"What is that supposed to mean?" said Kassim, his voice tightening. His face had taken on a wary frown.

"Just what it sounds like!"

"So you're the double-crossing crook who pulled that jewel swindle tonight!" Eric blurted, unable to bottle up his own furious feelings any longer.

"That's right, buddy boy," said Barton with an insolent grin. "Got the ruby right here."

He plucked from his pocket the small box which Eric had left on the park refreshment counter. Opening it, he displayed a gold ring, crafted in the likeness of twin coiled serpents with a huge fiery red stone clamped between their gaping jaws.

Alison could barely restrain a gasp of awed admiration. The enormous pigeon's-blood ruby glowed into the light like a mass of living flame!

Barton noticed her expression. "Pretty nice, huh, Cutie?"

"You're not from Hajar, are you?" Eric cut in.

"No way. Me, I'm just a little old businessman from New Jersey."

Eric Thorne's sapphire-blue eyes narrowed.

Meanwhile, a sudden light had just dawned in his sister's mind. "I'll bet you bugged the telephone in the royal limousine!" she blurted. "That's why you weren't worried we might tip off the police on the car phone!"

"Smart girl!"

"And that's also how you knew we were coming here tonight to check out the library lions!"

"Right again, Honey! And here's something I'll bet you *didn't* guess. We bugged your hotel suite, too. One way or another, we knew ahead of time every move you and the prince and his flunkies were gonna make!" Barton burst

144

into a hoarse, raucous laugh, delighted with his own cleverness.

"You certainly had an inside line to Hajar's U.N. delegation," Alison said tartly, with a scornful glance at Abu Kassim.

"What about me?" Al Ghazali growled at the gangster. "Where do I fit into your crooked deal?"

"You're strictly a bonus, pal. It's like this. Kassim here came to us with a smart idea. He knew the prince's old man had just bought a two-million-buck ruby, and he also knew the kid would soon be flying over to the U.S.A. So he offered me a deal. If I'd get some of my boys to kidnap His Highness, Kassim said he could supply all the inside info we needed to plan the snatch. Then after we collected the ruby as ransom, the other half of the deal was for us to turn the prince over to him as a political hostage, so he could force Emir What's-His-Name to step down from the throne. Well, natch, I don't take nobody's word for nothing when it comes to planning big jobs, so I told him I'd have to think it over."

Barton's first move, he explained, after taking time "to think it over," had been to send one of his mob stooges—the baldheaded gunman named Monk Macy—to check out Kassim's story that Prince Haroun's first stop on arriving in America would be the mansion *El Gezirah*, which his father was about to purchase.

Macy's regular occupation was that of bookmaker, a professional bet-taker on horse racing and other sports events. Calling the Ludlow Realty Company, he had pretended to be interested in buying the mansion for himself.

While the real estate agent, Fred Jessup, was showing him the house, Macy had drawn him into conversation about the unnamed wealthy Arab who was also interested in buying *El Gezirah*. All the information provided by Kassim appeared to check out, including the fact that the famous running back of the Chicago Bears, Al Ghazali, was coming to inspect the house on behalf of the unknown Arab buyer.

Jessup in turn was excited to learn that Macy was a bookie. And suddenly he had proposed a clever scheme to win a lot of money on the outcome of the upcoming Chicago Bears-Detroit Lions game. Because of Ghazali's brilliant scoring record, the Bears would go into the game as heavy favorites.

Jessup had been told the secret of *El Gezirah* by an old uncle who'd once worked as a servant of Murdo McKee. This had given him the idea for his crooked scheme. By trapping Ghazali in the underground room and holding him there over the weekend, the plotters could drastically alter the point spread of the game and win a fortune on bets laid with other bookmakers before Ghazali's disappearance became known.

The idea sounded foolproof to Monk Macy. Also to Barton, when Monk passed it on to his boss. They had decided to carry out Jessup's scheme without bothering to inform Kassim.

"See what I mean, pal, when I said you were a bonus?" Barton remarked to the football star with a chuckle. "A coupla hundred grand extra without hardly bothering to lift a finger!"

From Kassim, the crooks had learned that Prince Haroun and the Thorne twins would be coming in the royal limousine to meet the football star at *El Gezirah,* so they arranged to bug the car's telephone and plant a radio beeper under its chassis while the car was parked outside the mansion. This was done after the prince's party had gone inside, and the gardener (an unexpected complication!) was also called in to answer questions.

The radio signal from the beeper would enable the crooks to anticipate the limousine's approach, set up the roadblock and pull off the kidnapping when the limousine drove away from the house. (It had also proved useful in tailing the limousine later on.)

Yusef's prompt evasive action, however, had foiled the kidnapping, so the crooks had to devise another plan, by which the prince was kidnapped from the Crescent Oil skyscraper.The sinister announcement during the Broadway show, and the eerie subway incident involving the spook with dark glasses and muttonchop whiskers had all been part of the plot to worry and mystify Haroun and the twins, thereby helping to persuade the prince to act on the anonymous phone call's advice and agree to the midnight rendezvous on the skyscraper.

Barton himself (the mobster confided proudly) had played the role of whiskered spook, as well as that of the magazine editor who had tricked Persia Palmer.

"Brilliant!" snapped Eric sarcastically after listening to the gangster's story. "But now that you've got the ruby, why bother going along with this creep?" Eric gestured to Kassim with a contemptuous jerk of his thumb. "Turn the prince over to him, and you'll not only have the FBI after you for kidnapping—you'll have the CIA, the Emir's agent's, and the whole U.S. government breathing down your necks!"

"You got a point there," Barton nodded. "And don't think I ain't considering that angle!"

Abu Kassim glanced sharply and uneasily at him. "What are you talking about, Barton?"

"About you, wise guy! Like the kid says, we already got the ruby. Who needs you? From here on, you're just bad news!" Kassim started to bluster and argue, but Jessup blurted in a loud, nervous voice, "Mr. Barton's right! Like it or not, there'll have to be a change of plans! When I told Monk Macy about this underground room, I didn't know you people were going to kidnap an Arab prince and bring him here! And I sure didn't know these kids would get in the act! Now that they've seen us, and they know all about both capers, it wrecks everything! We can't just let them go and expect them to act like nothing ever happened! . . . So what are we going to do? Somebody tell me that!"

A grim silence fell as the sweating real estate agent looked around frantically from face to face, seeking reassurance.

"Ya know something?" Barton remarked to his henchmen. "The poor guy's right. We can't let 'em go. Not any of 'em. They know too much. With these two kids and foreign royalty involved, we can't risk *any*body squawking!"

"Meaning what, Mr. Barton?" asked the gunman in the checked suit.

Barton's lips curved in a wolfish grin. "Meaning we'll hafta kill 'em all—natch!"

15 • *Button, Button!*

Fred Jessup paled and ran his tongue over dry lips. "You, uh, really think that's necessary, Mr. Barton? I mean, killing all these people?"

"You got a better idea?"

"Well . . . no, I suppose if that's the only way to make sure no one talks . . ."

"You know it, pal!" Barton chuckled again, and the sound made Alison's blood run cold. "Take it from me, it's the only way."

Kassim shrieked suddenly at the real estate agent. "You fool! Don't you realize what he means? He is not just talking about the prince and his friends—*they intend to kill us too!*"

Jessup's jaw dropped open in a spasm of terror. But Barton was more concerned about Kassim. "Grab him!" he snarled at one of his henchmen. "But watch yourself—he may be carrying a piece!"

While Monk Macy held the other prisoners covered, the check-suited gunman rammed his revolver into Kassim's belly. He made him face the wall with his hands up and hastily frisked him. As it turned out, the Arab was carrying a small automatic, which the gunman deftly extracted from his shoulder holster.

Jessup had watched all this in a state of quivering fright. Now he began to cry out hysterically. The check-suited gunman threatened to strike him with the pistol, and he sank back into a corner, whimpering.

Then the gangster picked up Yusef's fallen machine pistol. He flicked off the safety catch and aimed the weapon at the prisoners. "Just say the word, boss!" he remarked to Barton.

Eric felt his stomach turn over. Alison, too, was suddenly scared to the verge of panic. Scarcely realizing what they were doing, the twins reached out and touched each other's hand, twining fingers as they silently prayed for strength to face whatever lay ahead.

One thing was certain. They were not about to let themselves be mowed down passively. Now that each had regained a measure of calm, they were ready to seize the slightest chance of escape.

"Wait a minute!" the baldheaded crook spoke up suddenly. "We can't kill all these people like this! It's too messy."

"So what?"

"Figure it out," Monk Macy told Barton. "Some of these people got important connections! An Arab prince—and Ghazali there, he's a big football star. You think if they disappear, someone ain't gonna start looking for answers? Once the Feds get into the act, this is the first place they'll search. They'll take the house apart right down to the foundations if they have to. And suppose they find a bunch of bullet-riddled corpses down here—then the heat'll *really* be on!"

Barton frowned and took out a cigar, which he punctured at one end before clamping it between his jaws. "Like I said—you got a better idea?"

"Yeah, I think maybe I do. Why don't we just burn the

whole place down? If we torch it right, nobody can ever prove it didn't catch fire accidentally. Then if their bodies ever are found down here, it'll look like they got trapped and burned to death before they could get out!"

Barton mulled this over. His face brightened. "That's smart, Monk. Real smart! OK, we'll play it your way—but let's get cooking fast!"

He burst out laughing and repeated, "Cooking! Get it? That's a hot one, huh?" Then his face turned serious again. "By the way, how do we get outta this firetrap?"

"No problem, boss," said Macy. "Jessup showed me all the angles when we first set up this caper."

He pressed a button in the carved molding that ran around the wall of the room at the top of the wainscoting. The metal door slid open and the light flashed on again over the stone steps. "That button I just pressed opens the bookcase, too," Macy added. Suddenly his expression changed to a look of annoyance and chagrin.

"Oh-oh!" muttered the check-suited crook as he caught on.

"Whatsa matter now?" growled Barton.

"I think Monk has goofed, boss." He pointed at the Thorne twins. "Look at those kids—they been taking it all in. Now they'll know how to get outta here after we leave!"

"Let 'em try. They'll get a faceful of lead!"

"Yeah, but we can't stand around waiting for 'em with our guns pointed at the bookcase till the whole joint's on fire!"

"Wait a minute," Macy cut in. "We'll pull a fuse!"

"Which one?"

"Who cares, we'll just keep yanking 'em all till we make sure that switch in the lion's eye don't work no more. Or pull the main circuit breaker, whatever. Once the juice is cut off, they *can't* get out—the door just won't open."

"Right on, Monk!" Barton nodded approvingly. "OK, let's go!" The gangsters exited up the stone steps, one by one.

The check-suited crook went last, keeping the prisoners covered with Yusef's machine pistol as he backed out of the room.

"Don't try anything, kiddies!" he mocked.

At the top of the stairs, he paused and told his bald-headed cohort to go and turn the lion's eye. Then as the bookcase swung shut again, he hollered down:

"Remember, I'll be standing up here with this burp gun aimed till the juice is off! If anyone pushes that button, I'll blast all of ya!"

The bookcase closed and the stairway light went out. The downstairs metal door also began sliding shut.

The grim silence that followed was broken as Al Ghazali exclaimed, "Everyone move clear of the doorway! Then I'll push the button. If none of us is in sight, he won't be able to shoot from up there—he'll have to come down to spot us and take aim. And when he shows up in the doorway, maybe I can break a chair over his head!"

Eric grinned, but not very hopefully. "Why should he bother coming down here? He'll just keep turning the lion's eye back and forth, and shut the bookcase again."

"What if one of us keeps a finger on the button?" Yusef proposed. "Perhaps he will not be *able* to close the bookcase or the door as long as the open-button is pressed down."

"Maybe not, but what happens if the rest of us try dashing upstairs? He'll still be standing there with the burp gun!"

"Wait!" Alison broke in impatiently. "Never mind all that—I think I have a better idea!"

Prince Haroun glanced at her with respect. "Let us hear it by all means!"

She turned to Jessup, who was still huddled in the corner. "Is there another way out, besides the way we came in?"

Jessup said nothing, but shrugged and shook his head.

"We know that one of the people who got trapped in

here was later found wandering in the woods, out of his mind," said Alison, turning back to the others. "That means *there must be another way out!*"

Eric's eyes narrowed thoughtfully. "Hey that's right! You mean a way that leads directly outdoors instead of up into the library."

"Exactly! And it makes sense, doesn't it, from old Murdo McKee's viewpoint? That way, he'd not only have a hideout down here—he'd be able to slip in or out of the house whenever he wanted to, without anyone seeing him!"

"It does indeed make sense." Haroun agreed. "In fact my father had considered having a secret passageway from his palace constructed for the same reason."

"OK, I'm convinced," said Eric. "But so far I only see the one doorway. Where is the other escape exit?"

"It must be secret, obviously," Alison reasoned. "That's why the servant and the workman who got trapped down here couldn't get out till Murdo came home and let them out. He probably didn't want to make it easy for a snooper to escape—not till he could take charge of the situation and bribe them not to talk."

"Any ideas where to look?"

"Maybe!" Alison pointed to the wall. "The same McKee coat-of-arms that we saw upstairs is carved into the molding. Not just once—the design's repeated over and over again, all around the room. And this push button is painted dark brown to match the color of the wood, so you'd hardly notice it unless you knew just where to look."

"So?"

"If you'll notice, brother dear, the coat-of-arms just above the button shows a key instead of a sword—just like the coat-of-arms on the right-hand lion in the library."

"Wow!" Eric's face lit up with sudden hope and excitement. "If you're right, there may be another coat-of arms design with a key—and if there is, we'll find the outdoor push button right below it!"

"*May* be." Alison repeated cautiously.

Since neither Prince Haroun nor Al Ghazali had been present in the library when the twins discovered how to open the bookcase, the difference in the coat-of-arms had to be pointed out to them—one showing a mailed fist clutching a sword, the other a key.

As soon as the two understood, everyone began examining the carved molding around the room.

"We'd better search fast!" Eric urged. "Once those crooks pull the fuse, neither door will open, even if we do find the other push button!"

Even Abu Kassim and Fred Jessup joined in the search —the former sullen and faintly shamefaced, the latter still half-dazed and quaking with terror.

Tense moments flew by. Suddenly Al Ghazali yelled, "I've found it!"

He pointed to a coat-of-arms design which showed the mailed fist holding a key. Directly below it on the carved molding was a brown-painted push button!

"Try it!" cried Eric.

Ghazali stabbed the button with his forefinger. A creaking noise came from the kitchenette on their left. Eric ran to look. "There it is!" he pointed jubilantly.

A cupboard had just swung away from the wall!

The underground apartment was lit by several lamps and ceiling fixtures. As the rest of the group streamed into the kitchenette to join Eric, every light suddenly went out! The apartment was plunged into total darkness.

"You found it just in time!" Alison murmured breathlessly to Al Ghazali. "They must have pulled the fuse!"

"All we have to do now," said Eric, "is feel our way out."

"What did you see when the cupboard swung open?" asked Haroun. "Another flight of steps?"

"No, it looked more like a tunnel."

"I shall go first," declared Captain Yusef Said, gently but firmly shouldering his way forward.

"Here, maybe this will help," Jessup said timidly.

He snapped on his pipe lighter and handed it to Yusef. The guttering flame showed that Eric's report was correct. The opening behind the cupboard revealed a cement-floored, brick-walled passageway sloping gently upward.

One by one, the owners followed Yusef. After a hundred yards or so, the tunnel ended in a short flight of steps.

Yusef mounted the steps cautiously. Just above his head was a boxlike wooden recess in the ceiling, with a top that appeared to be hinged. He pushed on this and it swung open like a box lid.

A draft of cool night air came flooding into the tunnel!

"Hey, we made it!" said Al Ghazali.

Eric and Alison both murmured a silent prayer of thanks.

Yusef climbed out first, then lent each of the others a hand. As the twins emerged, they saw that the "box lid" was actually the seat of a wooden bench, in what appeared to be a garden summerhouse or gazebo! It was well screened on all sides by trees and shrubbery.

Meanwhile, Fred Jessup and the traitorous diplomatic aide, Abu Kassim, were the last to emerge from the tunnel. As they climbed out, they were roughly seized by Yusef and Al Ghazali. Jessup's belt was used to strap his right ankle tightly to Kassim's left ankle. Then each had his wrists tied behind him with lengths of the tough creeper vine that grew up the sides of the summerhouse.

Realizing the strength of the giant bodyguard and the brawny football player, both prisoners were wise enough not to resist.

Yusef looked around for a fallen tree branch. When he found one thick enough to use as a club, he handed it to Alison.

"Keep watch please, Miss Thorne, on these two contemptible evildoers. If either makes the slightest attempt to escape or cause trouble, hit him sharply on the head until he becomes quiet."

Alison smiled nervously. "Thank you, Captain Said, but I doubt that will be necessary."

"Take no chances, Miss Thorne!"

"All right. But what about you others?"

"We have work to do," Yusef responded tersely.

Al Ghazali, Eric and Prince Haroun followed as the huge Arab chauffeur-bodyguard headed back to *El Gezirah* at a swift jog trot. Beyond the trees and shrubbery of the vast garden area, the graceful Oriental mansion loomed clearly in the starlit darkness.

Apparently the crooks had succeeded in finding the fuses that controlled the flow of electricity to the underground chamber without having to open the main circuit breaker. A glow of light still came from the gated courtyard at the front of the house.

Yusef and his three commandos crept around the corner of the mansion for a closer look. Sprawling full length in the grass, they peered through the shrubbery that fringed the drive to see what was going on.

The answer soon became obvious. One at a time, the crooks came out through the entrance gateway. Each was carrying a ornamental vase or bowl, which he placed either under Al Ghazali's white Cadillac or the royal limousine. A few minutes later he would carry it back inside.

"They're draining the cars' gas tanks!" Eric hissed.

"Quite so," muttered Yusef, "and they will use the gasoline to ignite the curtains and other furnishings of the house. Let me handle this please—and perhaps Mr. Ghazali would be good enough to help."

During an interval while none of the crooks was outside the two darted up to the house and lay in wait on one side of the entrance gateway.

The check-suited gunman was the next one to emerge.

Yusef seized him in a steely grip and clamped a huge hand over his mouth to stifle any outcry.

Al Ghazali then relieved him of the bowl he was carrying and smashed it over his head. The gunman crumpled silently to the ground.

Monk Macy and Barton were dealt with in the same swift, efficient fashion, and all were disarmed.

Prince Haroun was annoyed not to have been allowed to take part in the action. Nevertheless, he good-naturedly accompanied Eric to the summerhouse to tell Alison that the situation was now well in hand. All three escorted the other two prisoners back to the mansion.

On reaching *El Gezirah,* they found the three mobsters trussed hand and foot, and propped up against the wall of the courtyard. Yusef was standing guard over them with his burp gun.

"Well done, Captain!" said Haroun.

"Thank you, Your Highness!" the huge chauffeur-bodyguard knelt to kiss the prince's hand.

"You're wonderful, Yusef!" cried Alison.

"He was, of course, merely carrying out my orders," Prince Haroun said coldly.

Eric gave a slight cough. "I, uh, guess it's time to call the police, eh?"

"No need," grinned Al Ghazali, who had just come out of the front door of the mansion after telephoning. "They're already on the way!"

On Sunday, less than two days later, the Thorne twins were seated on the fifty-yard line with their father, Prince Haroun, and Ed Bancroft, watching the Bears battle it out with the Lions. The State Department man had flown into Chicago not long before the game to report on the final wrap-up of the case against Vinnie Barton, his two mob

157

associates, and Fred Jessup, as well as Abu Kassim and several other Hajarite rebels, now under arrest in the United States, who had been helping the traitorous diplomatic aide plot the overthrow of the Emir's government. It was a brisk, gloriously sunny autumn afternoon, and the game was going not at all the way Jessup and Monk Macy had planned.

The Lions' burly linemen were battering holes in the Bears' defense as they clawed their way upfield in the fourth quarter and scored a field goal. But it was too late to do much good against the Bears' ground game. Al Ghazali had personally run for over a hundred yards and two touchdowns, and a receiver had caught a pass for a third—not to mention two field goals, which so far had run up the score to 27-10.

"Too bad for Jessup and Barton's people," grinned Ed Bancroft. "Those crooked bets they placed are going to cost them a fortune!"

"One thing Eric and I still can't figure out," said Alison. "Who stuck that white warning tab with the red skull and crossbones on my shoulder bag?"

"Kassim's wife," Ed Bancroft replied. "She was scared silly by the whole plot. When she couldn't talk Kassim out of it, she tried her best to foil the prince's kidnapping by slipping you that warning signal after you landed at LaGuardia."

"Poor lady," murmured Alison sympathetically.

Ed Bancroft shook his head. "I doubt if that's going to help her husband at all, but who knows? It might help her, of course. They probably won't prosecute her as a co-conspirator, even though she knew about the kidnapping plot beforehand."

"What about that reporter, Tom Peel?" asked Eric.

He chuckled drily, "That's a long story. He followed up on the case of that first museum visitor to disappear. While sightseeing in the museum, the poor guy noticed how the lion's eye seemed stuck on instead of carved out like the rest of its features. So he touched it out of curiosity and the bookcase opened. Getting out later was pure luck. He was pounding the walls one day, still hoping desperately that someone might hear him, and he happened to hit the door button just by chance."

"So that's how Peel found out the secret of *El Gezirah!*"

"Yep, that's how he learned how to get in and out of the underground room. And he decided to cash in on the secret."

Alison stared in amazement. "He sold the information to people who wanted to disappear."

"You guessed it! First a gangster in fear of his life, whom Peel knew had had a contract put out on him. Then a surgeon with a drinking problem, who was about to be sued and ruined over a botched operation. Also an actress who craved publicity and a businessman facing bankruptcy, who was about to be exposed as an embezzler who'd swindled both his stockholders and creditors."

"But what about Peel himself?" said Eric. "What was *he* so afraid of?"

"Barton's mob! They were the ones who'd put out the contract on that gangster who vanished in the mansion. When Barton learned about the secret room, he realized how his enemy had disappeared so neatly—and he also had a strong hunch that the newspaper reporter who was exploiting all those cases had probably set it up. So he ordered some of his goons to run Peel down with a truck. That's when Peel decided it might be healthy to duck out of town and lie low for a while!"

Eric whistled. "No wonder he was slinking around in disguise!"

"Of course Barton also didn't want to risk him tipping off Ludlow Realty or anyone else, and spoiling their plans."

"He certainly helped us with that code message about the library lions," said Alison.

Eric nodded. "Without him, we'd never have found the secret room."

"And if the twins," added Prince Haroun, "had not found the secret room, Al Ghazali and I might still be prisoners there!"

Just then the crowd in the football stadium erupted with a roar. Al Ghazali had caught a screen pass for the Bears and was now swivel-hipping his way down the field, racing toward the Detroit goal line!

Ed Bancroft chuckled. "Oh, I dunno, Prince. Looks like *nothing* can hold that guy Ghazali!"